John Buchan was born in 1875 in
Childhood holidays were spent in t
a great love. His passion for the Sc
in his writing. He was educated at Glasgow University and
Brasenose College, Oxford, where he was President of the
Union.

Called to the Bar in 1901, he became Lord Milner's assistant
private secretary in South Africa. In 1907 he was a publisher with
Nelson's. In World War I he was a *Times* correspondent at the
Front, an officer in the Intelligence Corps and adviser to the War
Cabinet. He was elected Conservative MP in one of the Scottish
Universities' seats in 1927 and was created Baron Tweedsmuir in
1935. From 1935 until his death in 1940 he was Governor
General of Canada.

Buchan is most famous for his adventure stories. High in
romance, these are peopled by a large cast of characters, of which
Richard Hannay is his best known. Hannay appears in *The
Thirty-nine Steps*. Alfred Hitchcock adapted it for the screen. A
TV series featured actor Robert Powell as Richard Hannay.

TITLES BY THE SAME AUTHOR
ALL PUBLISHED BY HOUSE OF STRATUS

FICTION

THE BLANKET OF THE DARK
CASTLE GAY
THE COURTS OF THE MORNING
THE DANCING FLOOR
THE FREE FISHERS
THE GAP IN THE CURTAIN
GREENMANTLE
GREY WEATHER
THE HALF-HEARTED
THE HOUSE OF THE FOUR WINDS
HUNTINGTOWER
THE ISLAND OF THE SHEEP
JOHN BURNET OF BARNS
A LOST LADY OF OLD YEARS
MIDWINTER
THE PATH OF THE KING
THE POWER-HOUSE
PRESTER JOHN
A PRINCE OF THE CAPTIVITY
THE RUNAGATES CLUB
SALUTE TO ADVENTURERS
THE SCHOLAR GIPSIES
SICK HEART RIVER
THE THIRTY-NINE STEPS
THE THREE HOSTAGES
THE WATCHER BY THE THRESHOLD
WITCH WOOD

NON-FICTION

AUGUSTUS
THE CLEARING HOUSE
GORDON AT KHARTOUM
JULIUS CAESAR
THE KING'S GRACE
THE MASSACRE OF GLENCOE
MONTROSE
OLIVER CROMWELL
SIR WALTER RALEIGH
SIR WALTER SCOTT

JOHN BUCHAN
THE LONG TRAVERSE

HOUSE OF
STRATUS

This edition published in 2001 by House of Stratus, an imprint of Stratus Holdings plc, 24c Old Burlington Street, London, W1X 1RL, UK.

www.houseofstratus.com

Typeset, printed and bound by House of Stratus.

A catalogue record for this book is available from the British Library.

ISBN 1-84232-778-X

CONTENTS

CHAPTER 1

The Long Traverse

The thicket of self-sown larches, tinged with a glory of devil's paintbrushes, ended on the scarp of the hill as if some giant plane had shaved it clean. Donald struggled untidily out of the covert, for he had missed the trail, and with a whoop cantered down the long turf slope, jumping the patches of juniper. In three minutes he had traversed the waterside fringe of birch and poplar and was on a broad beach of shingle, beyond which, like the mane of a wild horse, the white waters of the Manitou swung to the sea-pool.

This year he had come to Bellefleurs alone, and he was very proud. His family would follow in a week, and with two servants he was getting the camp ready for them. It was a tremendous adventure, since for seven days he would be, within limits, his own master. He could go to bed when he was sleepy, and get up when he woke, and swim when he felt inclined. The sailing dinghy was forbidden him, but nothing had been said about the river canoes. He had never yet caught a salmon, and the salmon rods were in his father's case, but he could try for a monster with his own little greenheart. He might even get as far as the Grand Lac de Mathtou, tucked far away in the hills...

There was a swirl at the tail of the pool above the rapids and his heart jumped, for he saw that it was a big fish.

An unpleasing recollection followed on the thrill. The sight of the moving salmon reminded him of an interview which had preceded his departure. His last term's school reports had been shocking, and his father had had a good deal to say about them.

Donald was not an academic success. He was a keen field naturalist, and for his age cast an uncommonly straight line. Like all his contemporaries, he knew a good deal about radio sets and automobile engines, and would joyfully tinker all day with any machine. He was a master of fluent, ungrammatical French, acquired in his holidays at Bellefleurs. But in orthodox schooling he was a hopeless laggard. His Latin was an outrage, he abhorred the name of mathematics, and what smattering of geography he possessed he owed to his postage-stamp collection. Literature, except for tales of pirates, left him cold. But in the past term it was in history that he had chiefly fallen down. "He seems to be quite unconscious of the past," his housemaster had written. "The world for him begins with the invention of the internal-combustion engine. All the centuries are telescoped into one hideous jumble. He actually believes that the Romans only left England at the Reformation." Donald remembered the beastly words, which he had not quite understood when they had been read aloud to him, in a tone of slow disgust.

His father had been very serious on this point, rather to Donald's surprise, for he had expected him to pounce on his deficiency in Latin. "If you don't know where you come from," he had said, "you will never know where you are, or where you are going." And then he had added something which had stuck in the boy's memory. "You are a fisherman. Well, you know that if your back cast is not good your forward cast will be a mess."

Donald would fain have kept his mind on the cruising salmon, but these words of his father's kept coming back to him. They seemed more convincing than the ordinary talk of patents and schoolmasters. He knew only too well the importance of a back cast and how difficult it was to get a good one when the larches crowded down to the river's edge.

He turned up the wide gravel shore, facing a gorgeous sunset which made the river flaming gold and the forest a conflagration. It was the most wonderful evening that he ever remembered. Though it was early July there were no black flies or mosquitoes about. That was a queer feature of the Manitou valley, for most of the neighbouring countryside seemed to be in the dominion of Beelzebub the God of Flies, and Petits Capucins, the next parish, was almost uninhabitable in summer.

But the Manitou was like no other river. Most of the neighbouring streams had peat-brown waters, but the Manitou's were gin-clear, the colour of the grey granite rocks. Also it was not one river, but many. For three miles up from the sea it swung in noble curves through a shallow valley of woods and meadows. That was Donald's father's salmon water, and there was no better on the continent. Beyond that was a waterfall, which fish could not climb, and then twenty miles of deep canyons and rapids, which a canoe well handled could descend. After that the Manitou split into feeders, one coming from the Grand Lac de Manitou, which was full of big trout. The main one flowed from a strange tableland of moss and scrub and berries, which only a few hunters had visited, and to which the caribou herds came in the fall. After that, beyond the Height of Land, there was no human dwelling between you and the Pole.

In the glow of the sunset Donald saw three figures in front of him, whose heads, being silhouetted against a shining pool of the river, seemed to be decked with aureoles. One was large and two were small, and they were moving slowly upstream along the shingle. Donald knew who they were. He broke into a trot, found a patch of sand where his boots were noiseless, and surprised one of the smaller figures by suddenly punching it between the shoulders.

The figure gasped, turned round and crowed with delight. "Donald!" it cried. "You have come back! Oh, I am glad!"

It was a boy about Donald's age, but half a head shorter, a slim, sunburnt child with sloe-black eyes. His name was Aristide Martel, and with him was his sister Simone, his elder by a year, whose crown of dark hair was on a level with Donald's sandy thatch. Both in winter would be robed like little Father Christmases in homespun blanket coats and thick stockings and fur caps; but in summer their dress was like a South Sea Islander's, the minimum required by convention. Face and neck and legs were brown as nuts and plentifully scratched by brambles. They were the children of Celestin Martel, who had a big farm on the mantelpiece of flat land above the beach, and whose forbears had come to Canada from Normandy when Louis XIV was King of France. Aristide was still at the village school, but soon he would go to the city and then to Laval, for he was destined for the law, like his great-uncle the judge. Simone had already gone from Bellefleurs to the Sisters at St Anne's, and was now home on her first summer holiday.

The tall figure was the *curé* of the parish, Father Laflamme, who was the brother of Madame Martel, and the uncle of Simone and Aristide. He was a man nearer sixty than fifty, as lean as a heron, and his face was tanned and furrowed by weather like the bark of an elm. A wonderful face it was, with its high cheekbones and aquiline nose, very grave in repose, but sometimes breaking into a winning smile, for if the mouth was stern the eyes were merry. Like all Quebec priests he wore the cassock, and, since he had a weakness in his left leg, his movement along the shingle was like the fluttering of a big dark, wounded bird.

Father Laflamme had been only four years in Bellefleurs. All his youth and early middle life had been spent in distant places, as far away as the Mackenzie river and the Barren Lands north of the Churchill. He had been a missionary priest, and his miraculous winter journeys with dog teams had become a legend in the Northland. Often he had coquetted with death, and his lame leg was a memento of an adventure when his canoe

4

capsized and he was carried over a waterfall and dashed on the rocks beneath. No man, it was said, knew the Indians as he did – Plains Crees, Wood Crees, Swamp Crees, Chippewyans, and even remote folk like Dogribs and Yellowknives. Now that he was at home in a civilised place his energy had not abated, for he took an interest in everything from the children's prayers to the introduction of better milk cows. The parish loved him but was slightly bewildered by his ways, for on a Thursday, which was his holiday in the week, he did not go visiting his brother priests, but limped through the woods, watching birds and flowers, about which he knew enough to fill a library. But all reverenced him, including his Bishop, who, during his annual visits, behaved to him as to a wise superior. Children and dogs adored him, and Simone and Aristide were inordinately proud of their uncle.

He laid a gnarled brown hand on Donald's head. "Bless you, my son," he said, "and what is your news from the great world? I will tell you mine. The snow geese this April found a new halting-place. Six miles east of Petits Capucins I saw ten thousand in the air at once."

This was exciting, but Donald only nodded. He knew what the next question would be. Grown-ups had a sad monotony in their conversation.

"How did you find school? Is there perhaps at last something that interests you?"

"No," said Donald. "I'm rotten at Latin – and I can't multiply right – and history! – that's a bore if you like."

"A bore!" said the priest. "I am surprised, for last summer I thought you had the makings of an historian. When I told you of the Hudson's Bay you remembered everything, and, indeed, corrected my memory."

"That was different. I couldn't help remembering that. But my goodness! those beastly Greeks and Romans – and the English parliaments – and the Fathers of Confederation!"

The priest laughed. "Why do you dislike the Fathers? They were your own Canadian people."

5

"How do you mean?" Donald asked, with a puzzled face.

Father Laflamme laughed again "I don't think that in your school they teach history very well."

The children seized upon Donald, one hanging on each arm, and a breathless confabulation began. Simone said little, for she felt that the new world of the Sisters at St Anne's needed a good deal of explanation before Donald would understand. But Aristide chattered happily about birds and beasts, and how he had shot the rapids of the Petit Manitou alone on a cedar log, and how he had made friends with a half-breed who knew the way to the almost mythical Rivière de l'Enfer and had promised to take him there... As for Donald, after a few eager enquiries about fishing, he had only one topic. The splendours of the motion pictures had captured his heart, and he had become a raging film fan.

Most boys in their early teens come suddenly on something which fires their imagination. To a few it is music; to many a book; but Donald was deaf to sweet airs, and he was an inconstant reader. The first films which he had seen had merely disgusted him with their languishing ladies and demented lovers, and the comedians had left him cold, for small boys do not laugh too readily. He was sceptical, too, of the circus exploits of cowboys and desperadoes. But he had lately seen pictures which had ravished his soul. He had witnessed the pomp and glory of the old French Court, and armoured men going into battle, Nelson at Trafalgar, and Drake attacking the Armada, and marvellous Romans racing their chariots in cities of white marble. His memory was a happy confusion of glowing pictures and sounding names. He laboured to describe their wonders to Simone and Aristide, who had never in their innocent lives been inside a cinema house. But he had much the same difficulty that Simone felt about the life at St Anne's. That splendid world was wholly outside his hearers' ken, and his bubbling enthusiasm could not bridge the gap.

"In spite of yourself you are a lover of the past. But one need not go to the motion pictures for these revelations. There are better ways."

Donald would have demanded an explanation from Father Laflamme, but a shout from Aristide distracted him. "Ho! there is old Negog!"

The boy scampered over the shingle to greet a figure descending from the riverside scrub.

It was a tall man wearing the garb of the summer woods – moccasins and old jean trousers, and a shirt of caribou skin so dressed as to be soft as velvet. His high-boned face was scarcely darker than Father Laflamme's, but he had the low forehead of the Indian and the deep-set eyes, slanted ever so little, which told of some far-off Asian origin. His long, straight black hair was tied behind his head with a deerskin fillet. Donald recognised his father's guide, and raced after Aristide.

Donald's father always said that Negog was the best fishing guide on the North American continent. He knew as if by instinct where salmon lay, and he was a superb gaffer. Also he was an expert white-water man and could work a canoe in rapids which would spell death to another. His name meant in the Montagnais tongue "Salmon-spear," but Negog was not a Montagnais. He was a Cree whose people had drifted eastward from the south-west corner of Hudson's Bay into the wild land between the bay and the Labrador. That had been the hunting-ground of his parents, but he himself had moved south until he had fetched up at Bellefleurs and found there his summer profession. But each fall he disappeared and did not return until the snow geese came up from Georgia. In winter he was a trapper whose lines were set in outland places, about the head waters of the Rupert and Eastmain rivers and as far as the Labrador border. Mushing with dog teams and tramping incredible miles in the long narrow Cree snowshoes, he had penetrated to places which no white man had ever seen. So Father Laflamme said, and Father Laflamme knew.

Negog had a solemn face and a rare, kindly smile. He was also a man of few words. Only to children would he talk, and sometimes, after a good day's fishing, to Donald's father. Then he would tell wonderful tales in his funny stilted English learned in a mission school. He spoke of the beasts of the Northland as if they were blood brothers, whom by an ancient "gentleman's agreement" he was permitted to kill within decent bounds; for your Indian trapper, knowing that his future livelihood depends upon moderation, will never deplete a district. Bear and fox, beaver and mink and fisher, he knew their ways like those of his own tribe. He could tell you of rivers so fierce that, compared with them, the great Peribonka was a sluggish canal, and of mysterious lakes hidden in trackless forests. One story used to give Donald nightmares. There was a lake, said Negog, so deep that it stretched down to Hell, where the devils lived. Sometimes a grey trout or an ouananiche, when hooked, would dive deep into the abyss, and there the devils devoured it, so that the fisherman drew up only the backbone and fleshless head with the line in the dead jaws.

Negog greeted the priest with a deep ceremonial bow which he accorded to few. Had he been wearing a war bonnet its feathers would have swept the ground. He was in one of his silent moods, and this the children recognised, for they left his side to dabble their feet in the seductive shallows of the river. The two men stood together, looking upstream to where the Manitou three miles off emerged from its canyon.

Now this is the way of the Manitou. It flows due south for most of its course, but just before it comes in sight of salt water, it makes a right-angled turn to the east. Therefore the two watchers looked straight into the sunset. There was no high land to hide the sun, only a low fir-clad ridge, and its slanting beams lit the river from end to end with a long trail of light. Each pool was a deep topaz, each shallow a ripple of pale gold. The colours were fading in the fast-coming twilight, but in their ebb they gave the scene a more delicate mystery so that it seemed outside the mortal world.

The Indian sniffed the light wind which brought the scent of pines from the hills.

"For a moon I think it blow from the west," he said, "and there will be no rain. Evenings will be bright like this. It is weather for *La Longue Traverse*."

"Doubtless," said the priest. "Only none of us are going to take the road."

"Not the road by feet. I mean *La Longue Traverse* of thinking that journeys backwards. For a week at sunset, perhaps two weeks, each pool will be the *Lac à l'Eau Dorée*."

Father Laflamme frowned and then turned sharp eyes on Negog. When he spoke it was in Cree, with the hard risping consonants and the broad vowels, which was the Indian's native speech.

"I have heard of it. Once I was shown it – in the swamp country of the Clearwater. It is a mystery which I cannot fathom. They say it is a secret known to your nation alone."

"Not to my nation. To my house." The Indian in his own tongue spoke with ease and dignity. "Long ago, before Christ came to the Cree people, my family was the priest-house, and some old things are remembered."

Father Laflamme was still frowning.

"It is magic, and the Church forbids magic."

"Nay, Father," said the Indian, "it is not magic. It is a power which in old days some had and some lacked, but which all admitted. Today Time is like this river here. You see the waters for an instant, but you cannot see whence they come or whither they go. But to some of our fathers Time at certain moments was a lake which could be scanned from end to end. To them all Time was one."

Father Laflamme laughed.

"That is what philosophers are now saying. But if Time is one, you can see the future as well as the past."

"We cannot see the things that are yet to be," said Negog emphatically. "That would make man like God. Once maybe, some few men had that gift, but not today. The further end of the lake is misty. The most to be seen is some little way down the trail of the past, and that is possible only for those of my own house – and for young children."

Father Laflamme shook his head.

"It sounds like a miracle, and miracles cannot be wrought by human hands."

"It is no miracle. It is a gift which God has given to a few of us. It is like reading a book, only it is a book which cannot lie."

"But you work some magic?"

"Not so. All that is needed is the clear pool with the setting sun on it, the *Eau Dorée*."

"No more?"

"I also make my fire. Of herbs. That is needed to prepare the mind of him who would make *La Longue Traverse*. Smells are the best guides to memories, and it is memories I would evoke. A man's mind is the mind also of his ancestors, and what they saw is hidden away somewhere in his heart."

"That is true."

"Listen, Father; the things that have been are everywhere about us. They are at the back of all our minds. If we can call up their spirits I will see what another father has seen, and another will see what was in my father's memory. Also they cling to certain places like a morning mist. We breathe them and eat them and drink them, and we do not know it. Yet sometimes it is possible to give knowledge."

The priest brooded for a little.

"The boy Donald is at a critical age," he said at last. "He is like an acorn tossed in a stream. If it is anchored on the shore to good soil it may grow into a strong tree."

The Indian nodded.

"You think as I think," the priest continued. "I am not concerned with Simone and Aristide, for they have that in their blood which binds them to the past. But the boy Donald needs roots. He has an imagination which kindles easily, and just now he is crazed about the motion pictures which they have in the cities. We shall do him a kindness if we can open the door behind him and show him his heritage."

"That was my thought," said Negog, "for I love the child as if he were my own, and to his father I owe all."

Meanwhile the children were happily skirmishing in the river shallows. The talk between Negog and Father Laflamme, which Donald did not hear and, if he had heard, would not have understood, was a momentous thing for him. It was to make that summer holiday at Bellefleurs an epoch in his life. Looking back, it seemed to him that its highlights were the catching of his first Arctic char and his first salmon, but the real marvels were Negog's doing, and of that he was quite unconscious. For true magic comes secretly and is not remembered; otherwise we should find the world too dismal when it had gone.

THE OLD LOVE

The little countries are shaped by men
      And moulded by human hands. –
But you cannot trace on my ancient face
      The scars of the little lands.
They come, they pass, like shadows on grass,
      Or a child's play on the sands.

Dawns and dusks and storms and suns
      Have spun my tapestry,
From the lakes of the South to the snows of the
            North,
      From the East to the Western sea,
Which lays its arts on my children's hearts,
      And brings them back to me.

Far they may travel and fine they may fare,
      And new loves come with the years;
But a scent or a sound will call them back,
      And my voice will speak in their ears,
And the old love, the deep love,
      Will dim their eyes with tears.

To each will come a remembered scene,
      Bright as in childhood's day;
Dearer than all that lies between
      Those blue hills far away.

They will remember the fragile Springs
    Ere the horn of Summer blows,
And the rapturous Falls when the year burns out
    In ashes of gold and rose,
And the Winters brimmed with essential light
    From the crystal heart of the snows. –

The tides run in from the opal seas
    Through the thousand isles of the West,
And the winds that ride the mountain side
    Ruffle the tall trees' crest –
Forests old when the world was young,
    And dark as a raven's breast.

Morning leaps o'er the Prairie deeps,
    Girdled with gold and fire;
In the hot noon the cornland sleeps,
    And the drowsy crickets choir; –
The dews fall, and the sun goes down
    To a fierce mid-ocean pyre.

In the wild hay mead the dun deer feed
    And the long hill-shadows lie;
The regiments of prick-eared firs
    March to the saffron sky;
There is no sound but the lap of the lake,
    And at even the loon's cry.

The cold Atlantic gnaws by my feet
    As a famished wolf at a bone,
The wind-blown terns old tales repeat
    Of sailormen dead and gone,
And the apple blossom and salt spray meet
    On the skirts of Blomidon.

Mile-wide rivers roll to the sea,
   And my lakes have an ocean's moods,
But the little streams are the streams for me
   That dance through the scented woods,
And by bar and shingle and crag and lea
   Make song in the solitudes.

Far and wide my children roam,
   And new loves come with the years,
But a scent or a sound will bring them home,
   And my voice will speak in their ears,
And the old love, the deep love,
   Will dim their eyes with tears.

CHAPTER 2

The Gold of Sagné

Once upon a time Donald had had a craze for minerals, not unnatural in the son of a famous mining engineer. He had been given a cabinet as a birthday present, and had stuffed it with the fruits of his amateur prospecting. With a geological hammer he had tapped every boulder around Bellefleurs, and had laboriously washed for gold the sands of the unfruitful Manitou. In the process he had picked up much curious knowledge. He knew the russet bloom on a rock face which meant iron, the greens and blues of copper, the rose-pink of silver, and the canary yellow of pitchblende. Also he carried in his pocket as a sort of mascot a sample of gold-beating quartz from a lode in the North of extreme richness. It was not much to look at, for it resembled nothing so much as a bit of frozen haggis.

All day he had ranged the countryside, his lunch in his pocket, with Simone and Aristide. First every corner of the farm had to be visited. Celestin Martel had his hay cut and coiled and was preparing to stack it. The little fields of wheat and oats had made good growth and were within a month of harvest. Joe Petit-Pont, shepherd, cattleman, and jack-of-all-trades, was already shearing the few sheep, whose wool would be spun and woven in the long winter months.

They inspected their favourite haunts in the woods, and Donald noted with approval that a bear had made his winter lair

15

in the cave which last year had been the headquarters of the pirate chief Blind Eye, the Terror of the St Lawrence. The afternoon was very hot and the children had swum in a warm pool of the Manitou, the salt water of the shore being still unpleasantly cold. Then they had arrived at the Martels' house for a late tea, with bread and butter and blueberry jam and the crispest cookies in the world.

The farmhouse was Donald's notion of a perfect dwelling. His father's lodge was fresh and spacious and smelt sweetly of new-cut timber, but Madame Martel's was a thing on an altogether higher plane. It had mystery and queer corners. The door was of oak two hundred years old, and had three windows on each side of it. It opened into a spacious chamber, raftered with beams from the great white pines which had once filled the valley. There was a hearth like a chapel, and above an array of muskets which may have done duty under Montcalm. There was a big, old spinning-wheel for wool and a small spinning-wheel for flax. This was dining-room, parlour, and workshop of the household, for in the far corner was a bench where Celestin, who was a handy man, played the part of carpenter, metal worker, and maker of *bottes sauvages*. The floor was of soft wood painted in some dark tint and varnished, and on it lay many bright-coloured, home-made rugs. Beyond was a spacious kitchen, and on either side guest-rooms, while a staircase in a corner led to a nest of upper bedrooms under the steep roof.

But the charm of the place to Donald was the bewitching smell. It never varied, and when he returned to Bellefleurs it came to his nostrils like the tang of salt to a man long homesick for the sea. Sometimes at school and at home he caught a suggestion of it, and it made him want to cry. It was too subtle to analyse, but there was cooking in it – reminiscences of Madame's famous pea soup and partridge-with-cabbage; burning logs, and old timber, and tobacco, and home-spun wool, and fresh-cut wood, and tar and paraffin and Lord knows what else; and fragrant whiffs of pine and salt from the out-of-doors.

"Monsieur Negogue come for you soon," Madame told Donald. All the parish gave the Indian the title of Monsieur. She insisted on speaking English when Donald was there, for the benefit of her offspring.

"Yeh! The sea trout may be in the Sea-pool." He dived into his pockets and produced a collection of oddments, including a battered fly-book, in which he sought furiously. "I don't believe I've got the right kind of fly for this weather. You want something to give'm dry. These things are like feather dusters."

Simone and Aristide looked on apathetically. They were not greatly interested in sea trout.

Madame cast a glance at the contents of Donald's pockets, displayed beside his tea-cup. "Monsieur Negogue he say you bring your lucky stone."

Donald held up the dingy mottled thing and regarded it critically.

"It's gold, you know," he told his hostess. "At least, it has gold in it, though it don't look much like it."

"It is like a cold sausage," said Madame.

"My father says it's like a frozen haggis. It comes from the Gloriana Mine away up in the North. There's acres of that stuff underground, and they dig it out like stones from a quarry. Gloriana is going to be the richest gold mine in the world."

"But you go fishing! What does Monsieur Negogue want with the little stone? The trout will not eat it."

Donald shovelled back the junk into his pocket, all but his fly-book, in which he was searching furiously when Negog appeared. The Indian stood like a statue in the open door, making no sound or sign, but everyone in the room was at once aware of his presence. Donald got hastily to his feet.

"Thank you very much for tea, Madame," he said. "Are Simone and Aristide coming?"

"No. They go down to the village to the feast-day of their cousin."

Donald retrieved his rod and net from a corner. "Come on, Negog. The sun will soon be off the Sea-pool."

"But not off the Priest's pool."

"The Priest's pool is no use. You said yourself that it was only good in a spate, and then only for salmon."

"I think that tonight it will be good," was the grave answer. "Have you your little lucky stone?"

"Yeh, but what do you want with it? We're not fishing for cod so that we need a sinker."

Donald could never walk down to the river; he always ran. But Negog's walking pace was easily as fast as his jerky rushes. He had been right in his guess; the Sea-pool was more than half in dusk, for a ridge of mountain shut off from it the westering sun. But the Priest's pool, a long canal-like stretch above a short rapid, was all molten gold. Not a ripple or flurry of wind disturbed its silence. Wherever the sea trout were, they were not there.

Donald regarded the place disdainfully while Negog busied himself in collecting bits of dead-wood from the shingle and twigs from the adjacent covert. Presently he had a little heap of fuel to which he added some dried herbs from his pocket.

"What on earth are you up to?" Donald demanded. "We don't need a smudge. There's not a fly in the landscape!"

"Yet I think a fire will be good."

The Indian put a match to the pile and then sprinkled on it a yellowish powder from a skin bag. Instantly a flame sprang up, a queer purple flame which changed suddenly to saffron. Donald's curiosity was roused, and he came over to watch it. Oddly enough there was scarcely any smoke, but there was an odour which did not come from pine or cedar – a harsh, bitter astringent smell which made the boy feel a little dizzy. It slightly confused his brain, but it seemed to wake all his senses to a special keenness. He smelled scents which he would normally have missed, of dried shingle, of the river water, of the meadow of wild hay on the farther bank, of a patch of resinous junipers on a near bluff. He seemed to hear, too, very distant sounds, like the ripple of the almost tideless Gulf a mile away, and the jingle of Monsieur Martel's cow-bells on the upland pasture. Negog had taken the lucky stone from Donald's pocket and had placed it in Donald's right hand, clasping the fingers over it.

"Look at the river!" the Indian said sharply.

Donald turned to the Manitou and slowly approached the edge of the golden trough. He was no longer thinking about sea trout.

He was looking at a motion picture, one without captions. He did not need any explanatory words, for he seemed to recognise each scene and to know precisely what it meant. What language was spoken did not matter, for, whatever it was, he understood it perfectly. Donald was always a little slow in getting the hang of the ordinary picture at the start, but here his comprehension was so complete and immediate that he might himself have been the producer.

Two men were sitting on a stone terrace. There was a glimpse of grey gables behind them, and small slotted windows, round which a big vine clustered. In front was a rough, much-trodden courtyard, and beyond it the bosky edge of a wood. But the trees were not so thickly set as to prevent shafts of the evening sun making a striped pattern on the earth of the yard.

The two men had a table between them on which were set wine and a dish of filberts. They seemed much of an age, but time had dealt differently with each. One, who wore rough country clothes and had the points of his breeches and doublet undone for comfort, was as lean as a crane, and his high-boned face was deeply weathered. His hair, though he was well on in middle life, was still thick and ungrizzled. Some form of rheumatism had bent his shoulders and given his neck a twist to the side, but he looked a man who could still play an active part in the field, or on shipboard, or on the world's highways. He spoke with a hard risp in his voice, after the fashion of Breton folk.

The other was shorter and plumper, but it was an unhealthy plumpness. His face was pale, as if he dwelt too much indoors. His head had once been tonsured, but a general baldness was overtaking him. He wore the dark gown of the scholar, which he had tucked up like an apron round his knees. His speech was softer and slower than that of his companion – the famous sing-song of Touraine.

A soldier and a priest, one would have labelled the two at first sight – and yet not quite a soldier or quite a priest. In each the commanding feature was the eyes. The former's were those of a leader of men, quick, eager, imperious. The latter's were those of a master of his own soul.

The man in the gown spoke.

"What imp prompted you, Jacques, to bury yourself here in a forest? An old sailorman should live within sight of the sea."

"Not so, my good Francis. In half an hour I can hobble to a little hill from which I get a prospect of salt water. But I have had enough of Neptune. A seaman spends his days being buffeted with spray, but at night he snores in a cubicle like a cupboard. This house of Limoilon is my cubicle, for I am old and drowsy."

The other laughed. "Like me you have eaten of the Herb Pantagruelion. My ship, like yours, has come to port. Poor Brother Francis Rabelais of the Orders of St Francis and St Benedict and St Hippocrates has been to Rome and is shrived of his errors. By the grace of the Pope he is now Curé of Meudon and St Christophe and in favour with God and man."

A kindly smile wrinkled the sailor's face.

"But you have not yet found your Abbey of Theleme, my friend. That is what we all spend our lives in seeking. We see its towers far away and waste our strength in straining towards them; but halfway the grave yawns for us. Perhaps it is as well, for such treasure is not for a single mortal. I and De Roberval have opened the trail and in each succeeding generation someone will carry it a little farther, so that one day at last God's purpose will be fulfilled."

"Beyond doubt the Herb Pantagruelion!" said Rabelais. "But tell me of that part of the Indies they call Canada." He turned his head to the house-wall on which had been hung the horns and mask of a big moose. "That is the deer you call the *tarande*, is it not?"

Jacques Cartier nodded. "Such is the Indian name."

"It looks like one of the beasts in St John's *Apocalypse*. If that is the common run of deer in your Canada, you will need a nation of Gargantuas to cope with them. How would a haunch of that venison taste, think you?"

"Do not speak of Canada," said Cartier. "Canada is only an outlier. The true empire is that of Sagné, which runs from the ocean to the sunset."

"You have seen this Sagné?"

"From afar off. At the Isle of Orleans and at Stadacona I heard of its wonders, and saw indeed the river which bears its name descending between mighty precipices to the sea. But from the mountain at Hochelaga I looked into its confines. North there were hills firred to the tops with forests, and west the valleys of great rivers – so great that compared to them your Loire is only a trickle."

"Did you find the Emperor?"

Cartier shook his head. "His home was twenty days distant. There was no time left me for the journey in the short Indian summer."

"And the gold? That is the first question we stay-at-homes ask of the adventurer."

Again Cartier shook his head, this time ruefully. "I brought back ten casks of it, and seven of silver, and seven quintals of precious stones. At least, so I fondly imagined. But the King's assayers find little value in the metal, and my jewels were but crystals. 'Diamonds of Canada' is now the word of reproach.

Little wonder, Francis. The treasures of that kingdom lie not at its fringes, but at the heart of it, and I never got near the heart. But beyond doubt the treasure is there. What I brought home was indubitably the Mother of Gold and the Mother of Silver, and where the Mother is the offspring is not far away."

He rose and limped into the house, whence he returned with a brass-bound chest which he opened with a key from a chain at his girdle. From it he took a handful of ore specimens.

"See," he said. "That is red copper, and that is lead; that is silver and also its Mother. And that is raw ore of gold."

(Donald recognised in the junk pieces of iron pyrites, and copper pyrites, and galena, and zinc blende.)

Cartier fingered the dingy oddments lovingly, scooping them up and dropping them from hand to hand. He replaced them in the chest, and took from it a little bag of chewed caribou skin, with writing on its soft white surface. He untied the mouth of it and extracted a stone exactly like that which Donald was now clutching. Part of it had become polished from friction, and Cartier wet his finger and moistened it so that it shone dully.

"What is that?" Rabelais asked. "Is the Philosopher's Stone found at last? It is like the sloughed skin of a snake."

"It is gold," said Cartier solemnly. "Or at any rate it is the clue to gold. You must know, Brother Francis, that gold is found commonly in the gravel of the streams, or in the rifts of the rocks. But to Hochelaga there came a man from the north, a priest and counsellor of the Emperor, and he told me of a place where gold had interpenetrated the rock so that it could be quarried like sandstone. He said that the secret of how to extract the metal had once been known to his people, but was now lost; that it once existed was proved by the great quantity of gold ornaments they possessed which could not have been fashioned from the slender dust and nuggets of the streams. He gave me this piece of gold rock."

Rabelais' eyes opened wide. "What do the assayers say?"

"I lent them the fragment, but they can make nothing of it. Their skill does not reach so far. Yet they are ready to admit that it might hold gold."

Cartier pointed to the skin bag. "This I leave to my descendants, and maybe some day fortune will smile on one of them and tell him the secret. See, I have written how to find the place. Fifteen days' journey from Hochelaga up the river of the Ottawa Indians to the lake which is called in their tongue Deep and Slow, and then five days overland through the forests towards the Pole star. Then a man will come to a land where gold is everywhere, not in dust or lode, but in the plain stone of the country. He who finds that will find a richer Indies than the King of Spain's."

The picture vanished; terrace, woodland, and evening sky became a shimmering mist in which only one material object showed, the skin bag containing the mottled stone.

The bag was now the cord which strung together a multitude of swiftly dissolving scenes... It was handled and talked over by two old ladies in starched coifs and wide skirts, and thereafter it lay on a shelf in a dark room, becoming a dingy object, so dingy that the writing on the skin could scarcely be read... Presently came visitors to the old house, and the bag, with other oddments left by Jacques Cartier, was taken to Paris. There learned men peered at it through glasses, and chipped bits from the stone, and a new bag of stout canvas was prepared and the lettering copied on vellum and attached to it... From Paris it journeyed into the deep country to a great château which was the home of the Marquis de Montmirail, the trusted counsellor of King Louis. There it had more dignified quarters and would now and then be brought into the great dining-hall, where splendid gentlemen spoke of it over their wine.

Then its fortunes changed. Somehow or other it had crossed the ocean and lay in the strong room of the Intendant, in a quaint little castled city, which Donald seemed to recognise as his own Quebec. A grave, weather-worn man who was the Sieur de Troyes was lent it, and carried it with him far up into the northern wilds, to the very shores of Hudson's Bay... It was back again in Quebec, in a new linen bag with fresh vellum for the writing, and it lay in a coffer in a vault, while cannon roared from the castle of St Louis...

After that the mist descended and the bag next appeared in the hands of a British soldier, a young ensign, Malcolm Fraser by name, who took it to his new house at Malbaie, and then to his newer house at Fraserville across the St Lawrence. There it was a disconsidered possession, lying dustily on a shelf in the seigneur's little book-room, till a cadet of the family, bound for the University of Edinburgh, annexed it as a curio and took it again across the Atlantic.

In Scotland it had better treatment. It came into the possession of a certain Professor of Natural Philosophy, who kept it in his cabinet in his house in George Square. His grandson, who was a man with business in the Americas, showed it to a friend, a Director of the Hudson's Bay Company, who had a new bag made for it and new lettering. He went further, for once more chips were taken from the stone and sent to the metallurgists, who seemed to find matter of interest in them, for a memorandum was prepared on the subject and submitted to a Directors' meeting. But nothing happened, and the bag found lodgement in a Border country house, where it lay until two young kinsmen of the family, set on its track by the memorandum, discovered it and took it into their keeping...

Once again it seemed that the bag crossed the Atlantic. Donald saw it in Quebec – now very much the city which he knew – and then journeying up the Ottawa river on the road De Troyes had taken...

The mist came down, and when it cleared he was looking at a winter camp among snow-laden pines with, before it, the flat white surface of a lake. The swift panorama had slowed down and he was given a set-piece.

There were three men round the fire, dressed roughly like lumberjacks, with fur bonnets pulled over their ears, since it was forty below. Two wore Hudson's Bay blanket coats, and one a coarse woollen mackinaw. They had finished their supper of fried ham and flapjacks and tea, and had their pipes lit.

"Tomorrow," said the wearer of the mackinaw, "we will know the best or the worst. Our shaft is down to the reef – if there is a reef."

He took from his pocket a very dirty canvas bag and spilled a bit of rock into his hand.

"There's our talisman, or whatever you call it. If the thing is a wash-out, I'll have it ground to powder... No, I won't!... I'm bound to keep it as a reminder of the two best fellows God ever made."

"Tell us about the Hope boys, Shirras," said one of the others.

"There isn't much to tell. They were two brothers, Scotch, and this stone and the bit of writing had come down to them through their family. They hadn't long left school, but they had studied metallurgy some, and had gotten a notion that they had a clue to something big. I struck them at Toronto, and, having just finished a mining course at the Boston Tech. I was ready for a spell of prospecting. We took our bearings from Temiskaming – that's the Indian for Deep and Slow, the name of the lake in the script. Well, we pushed north, and got badly eaten by flies, and came to this lake, where we decided to start work. That was early in August '14. We had not begun when word came of the war in Europe, and the Hopes were off next morning like a brace of wild duck. Being an American citizen, it didn't concern me, but I felt sort of lonesome without them, and decided to put off my prospecting job. They left me the bag and the stone to do what I liked with. I guess they knew they wouldn't come back."

"They didn't?"

"Nope. Both got done in the first year. They may have been green, but, by God, they weren't yellow. When I heard of their

25

deaths I got restless and joined up with the French in the Escadille Lafayette. That old war didn't do me any good."

Shirras stuck out his left leg which was shorter by some inches than his right.

"This show is theirs as well as ours," he said. "If we get a mine it's going to be called the Hope-Shirras."

The picture blurred, but cleared again. It showed the cold light of a winter afternoon. Out of a hole in the earth a man emerged. In his hand were some fragments of mottled rock which he laid on the snow, and from his pocket he drew the bag and the stone.

"The dead spit," he said, and his voice was solemn.

The others had joined him with excited faces. "We've got to have the report from the mine office before we can be sure," said one.

"Yep," said Shirras, "but I've a hunch that it's all right. Say, Dick! get the pannikins out of the tent. There's a drop of whisky left, and we're going to drink to the Hope boys and the old birds long before them that started this racket."

The set picture faded and the panorama began again... Again it was a winter day, but the bush had gone. In its place was a town, with street-cars, and tall buildings, and the slim headgear of mines. Aeroplanes equipped with skis were landing on the frozen lake... In a huge mill quantities of mottled rock were being ground to a fine dust... In a stifling furnace-room ingots of pale gold were being moulded...

Then came the sound of speech and the scene seemed to be laid in a great city, in a room where many people were congregated. Someone was speaking, and snatches of his voice could be heard... "No longer a speculation but an industry... The Hope-Shirras, Canada's foremost gold-mine... Canada, now third of the world's gold producers and destined one day to be the first."

Donald rubbed his eyes. Staring into the pool had made him a little dizzy. He had no memory of anything except the sunset light. It was time to look after the sea trout at the river mouth. Negog had stopped attending to his little fire and was looking at him curiously. The saffron tint was just going out of the flame, so the reverie by the waterside could only have lasted for a second or two.

THE FORERUNNERS

You may follow far in the blue-goose track
    To the lands where spring is in mid-July;
You may cross to the unmapped mountains' back,
    To lakes unscanned by the trapper's eye.
You may trace to its lair the soft Chinook,
    And the North Wind trail to the Barrens' floor;
But you'll always find, or I'm much mistook,
    That some old Frenchman's done it before.

You may spirit wealth from despised dust,
    Gold from the refuse and gems from the spoil;
You may draw new power from the torrent's thrust,
    And bend to your use the ocean's toil;
You may pierce to Nature's innermost nook,
    And pluck the heart of her secret lore;
But you'll always find, or I'm much mistook,
    That some old Frenchman's done it before.

You may hunt all day for the fitting word,
    The aptest phrase and the rightful tune,
Beating the wood for the magic bird,
    Dredging the pond to find the moon.
And when you escape (in the perfect book)
    From the little less and the little more,
You're sure to find, or I'm much mistook,
    That some old Frenchman's done it before.

CHAPTER 3

The Wonderful Beaches

Next day Negog took the sailing dory and went down the river to Petits Capucins to see the carpenter there, a famous man, one Narcisse Jobin, about a new coble for the Manitou ferry. Narcisse was the best builder of boats on the St Lawrence, as good as any in Cape Breton or Halifax, but he was a difficult fellow to deal with, being odd in his temper and uncertain in his habits. It was said his father had killed a bear in the mountains and omitted the proper ceremonies; and that thereafter he had been a little mad and had transmitted this frailty to his son. Anyhow, Narcisse had to be approached carefully and coaxed into any job. To an order by letter or casual word of mouth he paid not the slightest attention.

Negog and Donald pushed off on a fine June morning, with a wind blowing upstream which would bring them swiftly home in the afternoon. They had to tack far out in the river to make Petits Capucins, so they saw little of the curious northern shore. Donald knew all about that shore, for his father had told him the story. It is written in the Flatey Book of the Icelanders that four years after Leif the Lucky had discovered the coast of Maine another company sailed out of Greenland with Thorfinn Karlsevni at its head. They sailed first to the island of Disko, and then south to the Labrador, which they called Flatstoneland, because of the great reefs on the shore. Then they came to the

29

Belle Isle Strait and turned west into the Gulf, passing north of Anticosti till they reached Petits Capucins, where they wintered in considerable distress. They called the place Furdurstrandir, the "Wonderful Beaches." This at any rate was the way Donald's father read the story in the saga, and he knew a good deal about these things.

There was no doubt about the Beaches. They were there today as wonderful as ever, a good place for a picnic on a spring afternoon. For nearly four miles there was a space of about a quarter of a mile between the wooded cliffs of the mainland and the river, and all that space was filled with great banks and dunes of shingle, with a selvedge of fine sand at the water's edge. It was a splendid place for sea trout, and this was the season for them, for the moon was full. Donald had brought his rod and a variety of double-hooked lures and hoped to induce Negog to tarry on the way home.

The visit to Petits Capucins was a lengthy business. Narcisse was in a bad temper, for the night before he had been revelling. He had been with his friend P'eitsie Leblond and had drunk far too much *bagosse* – a fearsome brew of "whisky blanc" (which is raw spirits) in which a beaver's tail has been steeped. The result was that he had a headache and was more difficult than usual. Donald left Negog conducting the slow negotiations, and went down to the mouth of the little Capucins river to watch the sea trout. There he ate his sandwiches, and then found an eel-fisher who took him out to inspect his string of pots. It was not until after four o'clock that Negog appeared and the dory sailed for home.

The upstream wind carried them soon to the Beaches. There, to Donald's surprise, Negog made no objection to a halt for fishing. He let down a heavy stone as an anchor about twelve yards from the shore, where the water was some six feet deep. The breeze crisped the river and for half an hour Donald's new lure proved effective, and he achieved some satisfactory long casting. The sea trout in brackish water, if you fish with a light rod and fine tackle, will tax any angler's skill, and Donald was twice broken. But he had five fish, three of them over four pounds in weight, before they suddenly stopped taking.

For the next half-hour Donald cast in vain, and as he looked at the Beaches, yellow and umber in the evening light, he began to think of the old Norsemen who had once anchored there. There had been several galleys; long craft with high prows and sterns, each with double banks of oars, and stumpy masts with square sails – his father had once drawn a picture of them. They had been a big company, for they had come to look for a settlement, and they had cows on board which had scared the natives. These men had come to Greenland out of Norway, and, not content with crossing the broad Atlantic, had pushed on into the sunset. Had there ever been stouter hearts?

"Who do you think discovered America?" he asked Negog. But the Indian did not understand him.

"What people came here first?"

"My people have been here from the beginning," was the answer.

"Oh, I know that. But I mean, what Europeans? There was a wop called Columbus who gets the credit of it, but hundreds of years before him the Norsemen came here. They stuck it out all winter on these very beaches. It's too bad they're not more famous."

"Of that I know nothing," said Negog, who was pulling up the anchor. "I think we go ashore and eat supper. I have food, and much talking with Narcisse has made me hungry."

"What about the flies?" the boy asked. The Beaches were a notoriously bad place for these pests, not only the black fly, his special enemy, but the horrid little brutes like hot sand which the French call *bruleaux*, and the Indians "No-see-'ems."

"I make a fire," said Negog. "There will be no flies."

Negog had brought a good supper for the boy: sandwiches cut thick, the leg of a chicken, and a wedge of cake; he had also his own queer Indian food, into which Donald did not enquire. There was nothing to cook, but he lit a fire as a smudge, for the flies were beginning to come out of the undergrowth in the cliffs, scenting a human prey. He made his fire on the sand very near the water's edge, and Donald as he stood beside it, sniffed the same queer odour as on the previous night. He had a sandwich in his hand, but he did not begin on it, for his attention was caught by the eerie light on the river.

The setting sun had made the still water near the shore a band of pure gold. Donald's head was full of the Norsemen who a thousand years ago had made camp here and seen the snow cover the hills and the river solid ice from bank to bank. A comfortless time they must have had, with fish hard to come by, and the deer far away up in the mountains. He could picture the big, fair-haired, grey-eyed men, like a Swedish engineer who had been his father's friend, their cheeks hollow with hunger and their armour dull with frost. Cattle, too! How had the beasts wintered in this fodderless land?

And then suddenly in the gold depths of the water a picture appeared.

Three long shallow boats were being launched at a slip in a deep valley, where between the mountains lay a silver strip of firth. On the shore was a little town of wooden dwellings, black with smoke and weather, with one big building which was partly stone. There was a concourse of people at the tide's edge.

Donald knew all about the picture, though no one had told him. This was Hightown under Sunfell, thousands of miles away in the Norland country, and these were the Wick people whose king was Thorwald the Lucky. There was no blood on the rollers which launched the galleys, not even the blood of goats, for this was not a hosting for war, but a voyage of discovery. The tall man in command was called Hallward, who two years before had led an expedition to the West, and had found a habitable country. There he had left his wife and children and some of his folk, and was now returning with other settlers, and the usual settlers' gear.

Ploughs and harrows were taken aboard, and a little herd of the small black Norland cattle. Food, too, for the voyage – salted fish, and dried beef, and casks of strong ale. The thralls took their places at the thwarts, and then the old seaman Thorwolf Cranesfoot, who had often sailed the Western seas. Then came the adventurers, a dozen in all, five of them with wives and children – mostly young Bearsarks from the Shield Ring. Last came the leader, Hallward, an older man who alone wore byrnie and helm, since he was ceremonially bidding farewell to Thorwald the king...

The galleys turned a corner of hill and Donald could trace them as they made their way from the Norland sea to the Atlantic. They were miraculously lucky, for they had for most of their course a following wind, so that the broad sails were filled and the oats were shipped and lashed under the bulwarks, and the thralls could sit idle and play on knuckle-bones. Nor was there any need to sling the shields out-board, for they touched at no land and saw no other craft. Under Cranesfoot's guidance they avoided Snowland (as they called Iceland), and steered a course between Shetland and the Faeroes. None of the portents which were legendary among their people appeared to trouble them. Icebergs, indeed, they saw in plenty, but not the Curdled Sea, of which they had been told, and which looked like a river of milk and brought down dragons in its tides; or the terrible Sea-walls which were the edge of the world. At the end of the second month after leaving Hightown they turned the butt of Greenland and reached the little port called the Eastern Settlement. Men and cattle were lean and travel-worn, but only one cow had died...

It was now high summer. The little fleet did not tarry, but sailed due west on the course which Hallward had laid two years before. They had got in a fresh store of food in Greenland, but not much, for the Eastern Settlement was always on short commons. But now they were in closer touch with the land, and Hallward promised that soon they should have fine fare, juicy bear steaks and the pied ptarmigan of their own Norland hills. At first they had misty weather – "Ran is heating her ovens," said Cranesfoot the steersman; and then the wind blew from the northeast and carried them into the channel called Guanengagap, which led to what Hallward called the outer sea.

In that channel they had their first serious trouble. It was choked with pack-ice, which the gales had driven out of the Dark Sea. Sometimes under a shift of wind or a tide-rip the pack would break up and there would be open water for a mile or two, and then the ice would close down again on the galleys like a vice. Happily these were stoutly built with double sheaths, or they would have been crushed like a nut; as it was they were badly strained. For two weeks they wrestled through the pack, scarcely sleeping, for it was often necessary to lift the galleys out of a jam by sheer strength of muscle. The food, too, would have run short had they not found a bear on a floe, which they slew with their spears – a monstrous white beast whose ghost, said the women, followed them barking like a dog.

At last they came into open waters. On his former voyage Hallward had sailed a promontory on the western side, whence he followed the coast southward; but now, since he must go south, he chose to hug the eastern shore. But first it was imperative to land and see to the galleys. They ran them on to a low marshy beach, backed by thin woods of pine. There was no oak to be had for their repairs, so they had to be content with soft fir. But the young men went far into the woods and brought back deer – some like the Norland reindeer, and some of a white-tailed kind, smaller, but of excellent sweet flesh. Also they met some of the people of the land, short, square folk with slanting eyes, and skins the colour of a hazel nut, and marvellous white teeth. These were a peaceable and friendly race, and in no way scared by the white men. Their weapons were of copper and bone, and they joyfully bartered furs and skins for a few knives of steel. Soon the women of the party had made new clothes for themselves and their children – tunics of white caribou skin as soft as velvet, and hoods edged with wolverine – against the coming winter.

They made slow progress to the south end of the Dark Sea, for they had to tack against contrary winds. But they reached it at last in mid-August. The flies which had risen in the evenings like a grey mist at their first landing, had now utterly gone, but the sun was hot and the moist air languid. Cranesfoot had guided them well, for they had made landfall at the very point where on his former voyage Hallward had built a shelter for the galleys. This was a great barrow, which had been the work of six men for a fortnight. In the Norlands the inner chamber would have been of stone, but there was no stone in this land, so it was built of great rafters and baulks of white pine. Here the ocean-going galleys, well caulked and oiled, would be safe until the next voyage, for no wild beasts could break in, and no savage would guess what lay inside the dun, at the solid entrance of which Hallward wrote with fire certain sacred runes on a wooden shield. From the barrow they brought out the smaller boats, shallow things pointed at each end, in which they must continue their journey up the southern rivers. There were eight of these – two for the use of the cattle, attended by the neatherds, and two for baggage.

Here sickness fell upon the party and one of the women died. A fever seemed to come out of the marshes, and the teeth became loose in the head and the flesh soft and rotten. Hallward was forced to wait in camp, and it was ten days before a better diet, the berries of the woods and the blood of fresh-killed game restored the party to health. Meantime he put heart into the newcomers by talking of the land in the south, now less than a month away, which was to be their home.

He told of his first venture, when they had to spend a bitter winter on the shore of the Dark Sea, and when in spring a lean and feeble company followed the wild geese south. He told of the tracking to their source of north-flowing rivers through a mighty forest which he called Mirkwood; of lakes larger than any Norland firth; of one vast lake larger than the Norland Sea. He did not touch on the dangers and hardships of the road, for his business was encouragement. But he spoke eloquently of the country they had found beyond the inland sea. It was not like this, a mat of forests, nor was it like the Norland, a wilderness of barren hills. There were forests – mighty forests, not of pine only, but of oak and hard woods; there were lakes full of fish and wildfowl; above all there were great plains of fine grasses, where wandered in herds beyond number a huge shaggy beast bigger than any elk and sweeter to the tooth. The place was a garden, for in the rich soil oats and barley brought forth crops such as the Norlands had never seen. It was a peaceful land, for there were few men in it, only a handful of feeble savages who fled at the shaking of a spear.

There he had made a home – Fairholm was its name – in the meadows between the lakes, with the forest at the door. His wife was there, and six of the Shield Ring with their wives and children. They had built a great hall of timber with barns and granges, carved out their fields, sown and reaped their first crops. Now, with the cattle they had brought, there would be milk as well as flesh and fowl and the fruits of the earth... Hallward's imagination kindled. This was no barren domain like Snowland, where life would always be hard; no pauper hamlet like the Greenland places, but a home in a rich land where the summers were bountiful and the winters gentle. Some day it would be more than a settlement; it would be a kingdom, a new kingdom of the Wick folk in the land of the sunset... His hearers listened greedily, and their spirits rose.

The journey was resumed. Now there were frosts at night, and a fire on the shore was welcome. Food was plentiful for man and beast. Five of the little black cattle had died, since fodder had often been scanty on the voyage, but the remainder grew fat on the glades of wild hay which lay scattered in the forest. There was game of every sort, deer and bear, and birds like the Norland ryper, and a multitude of wild berries to sweeten the blood. The birds fell to their arrows, and the bigger animals to their spears, when by cunning stalking they had been manoeuvred into a cul-de-sac and forced to stand.

Once there was a great fight. There had been grizzlies on the shore of the Dark Sea – the Barrens grizzly, Donald had decided, for he was well up in Canadian big game – and on several occasions there had been hard struggles before the axe of one of the Bearsarks broke into the great neck, muscled as hard as steel. But at this stage of the journey there were only the small black and brown bears which a woman could have slain. Suddenly in a glade appeared a brute like a mountain, bigger than any grizzly, his fur chocolate shading to cinnamon, and his claws like sickles. It was Hallward himself who engaged the monster, and he had a tough fight of it, for before he gave it its death wound his shoulder had been laid open by a pat from its mighty paw... Donald recognised it as the Kodiak bear of Alaska, two thousand miles out of its modern bailliewick...

Another thing made him hold his breath. He saw, though the adventurers could not see it, a gathering of clans of little people around the travellers. They were a dwarfish race, Indians not Eskimos, but more mongoloid than the Indians of today. Their faces were not painted, and they had no feathers or wampum belts, but only coarse skin tunics and trousers. Their weapon was the bow, and their arrows were tipped with obsidian. It was plain they knew nothing of metals, not even of the Eskimo's copper.

So far they had not attacked, but they had shot arrows at long range into one of the cattle galleys and wounded a bull in the rump. The voyagers were conscious of their presence, for more than once they had caught a glimpse of dwarfish shadows among the trees. They called them the Skridfinns, and laughed at the thought of danger from such pygmies...

So far the pictures had followed each other like a panorama, but now they altered. The party had come up the Albany and the

Ogoki and had now to portage over some miles of forest and ridge to reach a south-flowing stream that led to Lake Nipigon. (Donald could follow their course as easily as if it had been traced on a map, and the ground seemed familiar to him, though he had never been within a thousand miles of it.) It was the route which Hallward had discovered in his first journey. The boy saw the company encamped in a clearing around three fires, the cattle tethered to scrub cedars. He saw, too, an ominous thing, for all the woods were thick with the little people. They had kept their distance when the galleys were on the streams, but now, on this neck of land, they seemed to have acquired a greater boldness and to be mustering for an ambush.

By the fire where Hallward sat there was much feasting, for that day deer had been killed. The ale brought from Norland had long ago been finished, so there was only water in the drinking horns.

"We will brew more and better ale when we get to Fairholm," the people said.

The nights of still frost had gone. A keen wind from the north was tossing the gold and scarlet of the woods, and the moon shone fitfully in a sky filled with racing clouds.

Arnwulf Shockhead, the Bearsark who was second in command, was in a merry mood. That day he had caught a huge Nipigon trout and boasted of it.

"I thought that, like Thor, I had hooked the Midgard Serpent," he chuckled.

But there were two silent in the company. One was old Cranesfoot, who, when they left the water which was his proper home, had taken to sortilege making. He had cast the sacred twigs and had apparently got a doubtful answer, but the others refused to be depressed.

"It was no proper sortilege," said one. "There should have been first the sacrifice of a black heifer."

"The twigs are weak things," said another. "For proper guidance one must hallow three ravens and take their word."

So the merry-making went on, but Hallward sat silent. He had been a silent man ever since the big bear had clawed his shoulder. Arnwulf sat beside him.

"Cranesfoot is wise," he said; "danger approaches us Wicking folk, danger and sorrow."

Arnwulf comforted him.

"Thor is on our side," he said. "The shears of the Norns are blunted for us. Have you not for the second time sailed beyond Gunbiorn's Reef, which folks said was the end of the world?"

"Skuld has us in his keeping," said Hallward, "but not all of us." He looked up at the sky. "See, the Shield Maidens ride to choose the dead. The High Gods will exact a price for our good fortune, and I think that price will be myself. Death is jogging my elbow, old friend. I do not know how it will come, but come it will. If I must go to the Howe of the Dead you have my orders. You will lead our people to Fairholm, for I have told you the road. There you will present to them my son Biorn, and let the oath of fealty be sworn to him, and the gold torque hammered on his arm. Man, I see the future as in a glass. The day of Ragnorok will dawn for me, but not for you. I have spoken."

Hallward lay down and slept peacefully until an hour before dawn. Then he rose, shook himself, flung the long hair from his brow, and peered into the half-lit forest. He had scarcely got himself into helm and byrnie when from the covert came a shower of arrows.

"The Skridfinns are on us!"

The cry awoke the camp and every man buckled on his harness. There was no need for the Shield Ring, for the dwarfish people did not dare to close with huge mailed men, armed with glittering steel; but they could shoot their arrows, which came like a mosquito cloud. The Bearsarks, keeping in line, pushed into the forest, and took toll of any laggard Skridfinn. Hallward went first, swinging his famous sword which men called Skullsplitter. It was like using a great axe to sharpen a stick. The attack flagged and died away, and from far off in the woods came the patter of fleeing moccasined feet, like the sound of wolves in the snow.

But Hallward had met his fate. The arrows fell harmlessly from byrnie and helm, but one had flown straight for his right eye and pierced his brain. Like a great tree uprooted in the mountains he lay on the carpet of ferns and blueberries...

The swift panorama began again. Donald saw a ravine between two rock bluffs just where the portage ended on the bank of a south-flowing river. A little chamber had been built of logs, and there the body of Hallward was laid, clad in helm and byrnie, with his sword Skullsplitter laid athwart his breast. A black heifer was sacrificed – Donald could sniff the slightly nauseous odour of burning hide and flesh – and as the smoke ascended to heaven Arnwulf repeated the burial rites of his people, and the company renewed the solemn oath of brotherhood, swearing by the Dew, the Eagle's path, and the valour of Thor. Had their leader died at sea his pyre would have been a galley launched flaming into the sunset; but on land his sepulchre was a Howe of the Dead. When all was over, earth was heaped on the wooden chamber, until a great barrow had been erected which filled the ground between the rock walls and the pass... Then the galleys were launched and, solemn and sad, the company went south to their promised land...

Then came a very different scene. It was still the pass, but centuries must have flown, for the form of the landscape was changed. It was a wider place, for much of the rock walls had crumbled into screes. The Howe of the Dead had shrunk, for an Indian trail had crossed it, and the feet of thousands during the ages had beaten it neatly flat.

There was a man working there with pick and shovel, a rough bearded fellow in larrikins and mackinaw. He had sunk a shaft on the side of the barrow and was now busy dragging something from the interior. First he brought out some fragments of rusty iron like a potsherd, then a bigger thing like the blade of a shovel. Finally he emerged with a long thin piece of metal, much corroded, with a cross-wise handle. He flung it on the ground and stared at it with puzzled eyes.

"Gee!" he said. "I guess that's some old guy's sword."

Donald saw that it was what remained of Skullsplitter.

The boy took his first bite at his sandwich and rubbed his eyes with the back of his hand. There was a splash ten yards off; the sea trout had begun to rise again. The wind was blowing the smoke of Negog's smudge the wrong way, and the black flies had got at Donald's temples and neck. The brutes were quick off the mark, he thought, for he had been scarcely a minute on shore.

Some weeks later Donald's father talked to his mother after dinner.

"That's a remarkable child of ours," he said. "He's hopeless at school, but he seems to have acquired some out-of-the-way knowledge. Yesterday he fairly staggered me. You know that some years ago down in Minnesota they found what seemed to be an inscription in runes – ordinary runes which can be read. It was almost impossible to believe them genuine, for it would mean that the Norsemen not only discovered Labrador and Nova Scotia and Maine, but managed to get into the heart of the continent. Well, the other day there was an extraordinary find north of Lake Nipigon. A prospector dug a hole in one of the portages and uncovered what must be the skeleton of a Viking – fragments of helm and byrnie and cuirass, and a very well-preserved sword. So here we have the old fellows in the very heart of Canada! Moreover, the pattern of the sword suggests that it is older by a century than Leif the Lucky. They have got the stuff in the Toronto Museum and are going to publish a full account of it. I told Donald this, for he has always been rather keen about the Vikings. What do you think he said?: 'I know. They came by Hudson's Bay and went up the Albany and the Ogoki. It was a chap called Hallward. They were going south of Superior – I guess to Minnesota.'

41

"Now I am positive I never mentioned these names to him and never spoke about the Minnesota find, and you know how much of an historian he is. When I asked him who told him this he got very red and said nobody. He just knew it. Has that child got second sight?

"Another thing puzzles me," he went on. "Donald knows that the old Iroquois name for the moose is *tarande* – he mentioned it quite casually the other day. Now that is right, but the only authority for it is Rabelais, who must have got it from Jacques Cartier. Where on earth did Donald get it? I haven't a copy of Rabelais, and if I had he couldn't read it."

THE SPIRIT OF THE NORTH

"This was the word of the wise women who spin among the hills – to follow the road the King of Erin rides, which is the road to the End of Days."

Born of the grey sea-shroud,
　　Born of the wind and spray
Where the long hills sink to the morning cloud,
　　And the mist lies low on the bay;
Child of the stars and the skies,
　　Child of the dawn and the rain,
The April shining of ladies' eyes,
　　And the infinite face of pain.

Seal on the hearts of the strong,
　　Guerdon thou of the brave,
To nerve the arm in the press of the throng,
　　To cheer the dark of the grave. –
Far from the heather hills,
　　Far from the misty sea,
Little it irks where a man may fall,
　　If he fall with his heart on thee.

To fail and not to faint,
　　To strive and not to attain,
To follow the path to the End of Days
　　Is the burden of thy strain.
Daughter of hope and tears,

Mother thou of the free,
As it was in the beginning of years,
And evermore shall be.

CHAPTER 4

Cadieux

Donald had a holiday task from school, and holiday tasks he regarded as an outrage upon the decencies of life. It was to master a collection of tales from Greek and Roman history. Now he had a peculiar distaste for those great classical peoples, especially the Romans, for it was in connection with the speech of that calamitous folk that he had suffered his worst academic disgraces. So he started out on the book without much hope of enjoyment. And suddenly he had found something which enthralled him, the story of Thermopylae. This was talking. That three hundred Spartans should have held up a million or so Persians, and upset all the plans of the Persian king, was a glorious thing to think about. Donald knew just how it happened. There were places along the St Lawrence, like Cap Tourmente, for example, where the hills dropped steeply into the sea, and a handful could defy a host.

He read the story after breakfast on the Sunday morning, and was so excited that he had to skip about the verandah of the camp. It promised to be a blistering hot day, and since there was nothing better to do he decided to go to church. Donald's family was latitudinarian in their devotions. At home they were Presbyterian, but at Bellefleurs his father on Sunday used to read the English Prayer Book, and quite often Donald accompanied the Martel family to the little white church with its silvered spire,

45

where Father Laflamme ministered. So that day he joined Simone and Aristide at Mass and sat reverently through a service of which he comprehended not one word, sniffing the scent of incense with a feeling that he was doing something rather adventurous. And all the time his heart within him was exulting over Thermopylae.

Wandering about after luncheon he found Father Laflamme basking in a chair in front of the presbytery and reading his breviary. Donald flung himself on the grass beside him, for Father Laflamme was good company whether he chose to talk or not. By and by the priest closed his book.

"Idle, Donald? What are your plans today?"

"None. Oh yes! I am going up the river with Negog this evening."

"Not to fish, I hope. Your father doesn't allow fishing on Sunday."

" 'Course not, but I want to look at the water. There's a big fish in Baptiste's Pool. Negog says I may have a try for him tomorrow."

"Until then you have nothing to do? Have you no book?"

"Yes. I was reading a book this morning. About the Greeks. I found the best story I've ever read – about the Spartan fellows that stuck up the Persians at a place called Thermopeily."

"You haven't got it right. It's Thermopylae. Yes, that's a pretty good story. There are many others like it, you know – a man, or a handful of men sacrificing their lives to save their country. We have a fine Canadian one. Did you ever hear about Dollard – Adam Dollard – or Daulac, as some call him?"

Donald had not.

"Some day, if you remind me, I'll tell you the whole story, for it's a long one. But here's the gist of it. It happened in May in the year 1660, when the French in Canada were hanging on by their eyelids. There were only a few thousands of them, and their enemies, the Iroquois, were mustering on all sides for an attack which was to wipe them out for good. That was before the King of France had sent any soldiers. The Indian plan was for a big army to go down the Ottawa and others to go down the Richelieu, while the forces which had devastated the Isle of Orleans waited in the east. So Quebec and Montreal would be enclosed on all sides.

"Well, the captain of the guard at Montreal was a young French soldier of twenty-five, Dollard, the Sieur des Ormeaux in France. He concluded that attack was the best kind of defence, so he got permission from the Governor, Maison-neuve, to go up the Ottawa river to a place called the Long Sault, where the rapids are. His plan was to attack the Iroquois as they came down the stream at a spot where they would be at a disadvantage. Sixteen young Frenchmen joined him, all under thirty, and like Crusaders, before they set out they confessed and received the Sacrament. They took an oath never to ask quarter.

"They reached the Long Sault in time and built a fort with palisades. Soon the Iroquois appeared and were greeted by a deadly volley. The Indians disembarked in a fury, built a fort of their own, and settled down to destroy Dollard, who, had been joined by a few Hurons and Algonquins. They fought for five days, while the Frenchmen suffered desperately from thirst and hunger. On the fifth day came the main attack, which was beaten off. But it could be only a question of time. In the end the savages rushed the place and Dollard died and all his little band. But he did not die in vain. The Iroquois had lost heavily and sat down to think. If seventeen Frenchmen, four Algonquins and one Huron, they argued, could hold up seven hundred of their best warriors for mote than a week behind a wooden palisade, what would happen if some hundreds of Frenchmen defended themselves behind walls of stone? The invaders melted away into the woods and Canada was saved."

Donald drew a long breath.

"Gosh!" he said. "That was as good as Thermopylae."

Father Laflamme smiled.

"It's a fine story. But I think I know a finer. After all, Dollard was a professional soldier. And he longed to be a martyr. He came to Canada to die – otherwise he would have gone to fall in the battles against the Turks. But there was once a Canadian who did the same kind of thing, and he had no hankerings after martyrdom. Did you ever hear of Cadieux?"

Donald shook his head.

"Cadieux – Cadieux de Courville." Father Laflamme repeated the name almost lovingly. "I have a peculiar liking for Cadieux. There wasn't much of the saint about him, and he certainly didn't want to be a martyr. He was a *coureur de bois* – you know about them – the adventurers who went to the back of beyond seeking furs and in their wanderings discovered Canada. Some of them were no better than outlaws and made any amount of trouble with the Indians, but most were decent fellows who preferred travelling the woods to working at a trade or driving a plough. Cadieux was the leader of his band of *coureurs*. There was nothing about woodcraft he did not know; he could follow a trail like an Indian, and no weather could stop him – a sort of Ulysses – a man of many shifts and devices. He was always laughing and he was always singing. Sometimes the songs would be the hymns of his childhood, like 'Mon petit Jésus, bonjour'; but more often they were love songs like La Rose Blanche; or nursery rhymes out of France, like 'Compagnons de la Marjolaine' or 'Trois petites Dorion'; or wild songs of the woods, like 'Tenaouich' Tenaga'. He was a poet, too, on his own account, and made at least one song which can never be forgotten.

"He was pious, this Cadieux, in his own way, though he did not go to church very often, since he lived mostly where there were no churches. He admired greatly the stout-hearted priest Dollier de Casson, who had been a cavalry officer under Turenne and could lay out any Indian brave with a blow of his fist, and in trouble he prayed much to St Anthony of Padua, who was his favourite saint. When he came back to Montreal from his winter's hunting he did not lie drunk, like many *coureurs*, until he had spent the price of his beaver skins or fracas about naked with a brandy keg under his arm. No, he would dance with the young girls and tell wonderful tales to the boys, and would play with the children. A *bon enfant* was this Cadieux, and all eyes followed him affectionately when he marched into town, with his fringed leggings, and embroidered shirt, and *ceinture flechée*, and an eagle plume in his beaded hat. There was no better-loved youth in all Canada."

Father Laflamme paused.

"I cannot tell you the story now, for I must go to the village to see Grandmother Gauthier, who is sick."

"But please tell me what happened to him," Donald begged.

"He died very nobly. He and his companions were returning from the west down the Ottawa river in the spring with a heavy load of furs. They fell in with a big band of Iroquois who had destroyed a French settlement on Lake Huron, and were now beating the forest for French hunters. This was after the time of Dollard, and Canada was no longer in danger of an Iroquois invasion, but there was always a risk to lonely settlements and isolated trappers and traders. Well, the *coureurs* had been able to slip through the Iroquois' net, but they were hotly pursued, and at Calumet island in the Ottawa the crisis came. If they could pass the rapids there they could reach the French settlements and safety. Cadieux had delayed the pursuit, but at the Calumet rapids the Indians were close on him and they must be stopped if his men were to pass. Alone he held up the enemy, and slew so many that the Iroquois retreated. But he got his death wound. When his comrades came back to look for him they found that he had dug his grave and was lying dead in it. Beside him lay a song which he had written on birch-bark. We still sing that swan song of the dead Cadieux. It begins:

'*Petit rocher de la haute montagne*
Je viens ici finir cette campagne.'"

Father Laflamme crooned the verse in his deep voice to a sad, eerie tune, which reminded Donald of the old songs of the Hebrides which his mother sometimes sang.

For the rest of the afternoon the melody rang in his head. He had not caught any of the lines, but the air was firm in his memory. He hummed it at tea-time, and he was still humming it when Negog and he strolled up the river to Baptiste's Pool. One queer thing happened. He set Negog humming it. Now an Indian does not sing; he howls. After his childhood there seems to be no tunefulness in his voice. But Negog was now making odd sounds just above his breath, and if there was little music in them they had the rhythm of Father Laflamme's song.

Beyond doubt there were salmon in Baptiste's Pool. One great fellow broke water near the other bank, and in the rapids at the top Donald could see moving fish. Tomorrow he decided he would have a try for them with his little greenheart trout-rod, and Heaven be kind to him if he hooked one.

But somehow the prospect did not greatly excite him. His head was still full of the stories of the day: Thermopylae, Dollard, and above all Cadieux. Cadieux's song, melancholy as a lost wind, sighed in his ears. Negog had not made a fire. He was sitting on a tussock of grass smoking his pipe and watching the boy as he wandered by the shingle.

Presently Donald came to a spit of rock which ran far out into the pool. Here the current of the Manitou was close to the farther shore, and between it and him was a stretch of still water, golden in the sunset. As Donald looked into the depths a picture shaped itself.

He was in the air, looking down from a great height on a wide landscape. It was one which he seemed to know, and yet did not know, for though the general lines of it were familiar the details were strange.

There could be no mistake about Quebec. The passing of time had not changed the line of the Laurentians in the north, the bold bluff of Cap Diamond or the shining waters which cradled the Isle of Orleans. Only there was less cultivated land in the St Charles valley, and the forest came closer to the shore. It was a shabby little town. There was a huddle of houses at the water's brink, and above on the peninsula, close to the edge of the rock, was a square fort, whose guns commanded the lower town and the river narrows. One side of the fort was the Château of St Louis, the Governor's residence, an ugly building of wood, with the *fleur de lys* drooping from the flagpole, and near it a tall new church, and the stone walls of the Ursuline Convent, the Hôtel Dieu, and Bishop Laval's Seminary. On the highest point of land, as a warning to evil-doers, stood a great gibbet with the bones of a dead felon in a cage.

Donald's viewpoint seemed at one moment to be high in the air, giving him a wide prospect, and at another close to the ground. The St Lawrence unveiled itself as he moved west. The woods crowded down to the water, but at Three Rivers there was a cluster of dwellings and a church inside a palisade. After that little farms began to dot the riverside, strung out like the beads in a ragged rosary – a shingled house and barn, a few fields of charred stumps with crops sown between, and then the mat of the forest. He had a clearer view now, and could pick out the rude wharves, the home-made boats at their moorings, the barefoot children playing in the mud – healthy little imps fed on rye bread and stewed eels. And everywhere he saw Indians moving freely in and out of the settlements; tame Hurons, for the most part, but now and then a swaggering figure from the warrior tribes of the south shore.

Presently he was looking down on Montreal. He knew that it was Montreal because of the Mountain, but it was very unlike the bustling city of his acquaintance. There was a line of small houses along the river, and the foreshadowing of a street, which in wet weather must have been like a muskeg. On the west side there was a fort, and on the east rose a huge windmill of stone enclosed in a wall loopholed for muskets. There was no palisade round the town, and Donald saw Indians in the streets who were not tame Hurons or Algonquins. He saw the Hôtel Dieu and the seminary of St Sulpice, both fortified for defence. Montreal had a frontier air. There were soldiers of the French regiment of Carignan lounging at the tavern doors, big fellows with looped hats and bandoliers. The men, too, in the streets had a touch of the wilderness in their air. They had the long stride of a folk accustomed to winter journeys on snow-shoes, and the keen eyes of those whose life hung on their vigilance; while they wore for the most part buckskin coats and fringed leggings, and in their caps tufts of turkey feathers. Donald knew that he was looking at the famed *coureurs de bois*.

The view was still unfolding itself. Now he had gone westward past Lake St Louis and the Lake of the Two Mountains, and was in the broad vale of the Ottawa. It was early May, the grass was already springing, and the young leaves of maple, birch, and poplar made a pale green shimmer among the dusk of the pines. Near the river was an occasional farm, and sometimes at the mouth of a tributary a palisaded village with its church and mill. And then there came a line of unbroken forest, stretching from the far Laurentians to the Ontario hills, and muffling the water's edge.

It was like looking down on an anthill and waiting for the ants to show themselves. The place seemed silent and dead, but Donald knew that somewhere it held a fierce life.

By and by he found what he sought.

Three canoes were coming down the river, big forty-foot canoes of the kind used for heavy transport. Amidships they were laden with pelts, in bales with the fur inside, the product of months of winter hunting. Till now they had had a prosperous voyage, no short commons of green berries, and Labrador tea and *tripe do roche*, but full meals of corn and venison, and in Lent they had eaten beaver tails, which, since the beaver is an aquatic beast, were permitted fare. The crews, fifteen in all, were ten white *voyageurs*, four Hurons, and one Récollet friar, Father

Anastase, who had been picked up in the woods west of Lake Nipissing, a fugitive from a mission which the Iroquois had destroyed. The priest was in a sad state; his feet were so blistered that it was agony to put them to the ground; his brown Franciscan robe was in tatters, and in the place of a cord he had a length of grapevine. But he was not the least cheerful of the party, and he hugged the treasures which he had rescued from the burning mission, a picture of St Ignatius, and another of Our Lady of Pity surrounded by the five wounds of her son. As the men plied their paddles they were always casting glances behind them. When they landed on a spit of land to eat a meal of Indian porridge and dried venison, they seemed in a fever to be off again. Clearly there was some deadly peril in their rear.

But the company were in no panic. Their brown faces were solemn, but as composed as if they had been in the Montreal streets. Donald knew their names. There were Du Gay and Pepin from Montreal, and young La Violette from Three Rivers, and Jean Poncet from the lower Ottawa, who knew the country best, and Nicholas Brulé, so called because he had once been tortured at an Indian stake. There was a lean tow-headed youth, whom they called Jemme Anglais – English Jim – who had made the English colonies too hot to hold him and had skipped over the border. But especially there was a short fellow with a merry face and immense breadth of shoulder, with the pale eyes of the marksman and the stout calves of one whose legs were trained for the winter woods. In that silent company he alone gave tongue, for he was always humming or singing, and often his laugh rang out as gay as a child's. He was the leader of the band, for he gave the orders... Donald knew that he was looking at the famous Cadieux.

"In five hours we reach the Calumet rapids," he said. "After that we are safe, for at Merciet's Mill there is a strong stockade and twenty stout lads to hold it."

"What about the portage?" one asked. "That's a difficult business, and the Iroquois will overtake us there."

"There must be no portage," was the answer. "We must shoot the rapids. Jean Poncet is a good white-water man and will bring us through. He goes bowsman in the first canoe and you others must follow his steering."

The priest spoke up. "They have the pace of us," he said. "They have birch-bark canoes, lightly laden. I fear they will be upon us before Calumet."

"They may be delayed," said Cadieux.

"It will be a narrow thing," said English Jim. "I have a horrid tingling at the roots of my hair." He glanced at the Récollet, whom he liked to chaff, for he came of Puritan stock. "I am in the mood to make a pact with Satan and cry, '*Acabri, Acabra, Acabram!*' if he will give us a passage in his *chasse-galerie.*"

The Father frowned. "Peace, my son! The Devil's flying-boat would take us not to Mercier's Mill but to Hell."

"Better a cheerful hell than an Indian stake," was the answer.

As they pushed off Cadieux remained behind.

"Good speed, my brave ones," he cried. "Don't touch land again until you are past Calumet. Follow Poncet close, for he is your hope of salvation."

"What about yourself?" one asked.

"I stay behind to guard your rear."

"You're crazy, captain," Du Gay cried. "What can you do against a hundred howling wolves?"

Cadieux grinned. "I have already done something. I have visited their camp and burnt two of their canoes, besides scaring them into fits with my ghost drum. That meant half a day's grace... I have stripped the bark from a tree and drawn on the trunk their own pictures so that they thought a rival band of Senecas was ahead of them, and waited for hours to send out scouts to enquire."

"What start do you reckon we have?" English Jim asked.

"An hour, maybe. Not more. If they come upon us before Calumet we shall not make the rapids. They have muskets from Albany – God's malison on the Dutch! – and can blow us out of the water. Therefore they must not get beyond the start of the portage."

"For the love of Christ, Cadieux," young La Violette cried, "don't go hunting for death. Come with us. If need be let's go to Heaven together."

Cadieux's only answer was a laugh. "*En avant!* my children. I have my task and you have yours. We shall soon drink together at Mercier's Mill," and he waved his hand and turned into the woods.

The canoes passed at the bend of the river, and Donald's eyes looked eagerly westward. His heart nearly stopped beating when he caught sight of the pursuit. An hour behind! They were scarcely thirty minutes. For a moment he had a long view into the back country, up the Ottawa and west to Lake Nipissing and the French river and Georgian Bay. He saw the still smoking ruins of the Huron mission. He saw the trail of the Iroquois, the bark houses which they built each night, for they did not use teepees. He saw dead men in the woods, scalpless and horrible. And then he saw the fleet of war canoes slipping down the stream like a young brood of mallards.

He discovered Cadieux. The *courour de bois* had found shelter in a clump of reeds close to the shore, at a bend in the river where it was broken by an island and the main stream made a right-angled turn. There was something magical about Donald's eyesight or he would never have detected Cadieux, so cunningly was he hidden. He noticed that his musket was laid so as to command the passage.

The flotilla swung downstream with a great shouting, for the Iroquois thought that any need for secrecy was past, and that their quarry was already in their hands. Donald's blood chilled as he looked at them, for he had never imagined a more terrible sight. All were young, and, since they were on the warpath, they were mostly mother-naked. There were a few in shirts of deerskin fringed with porcupine quills, and one or two wore old-fashioned corslets of twigs interlaced with hempen cords. All were painted and oiled, their muscles suppled by rubbing with the fat of the wild cat. Their breasts were tattooed in strange patterns, and their faces scored with red paint in concentric rings. Out of the paint their small eyes gleamed like a ferret's. Their heads were shaven, except for a top-knot in which eagle feathers were stuck. They kept time to their paddles with a wild rhythmic tune which broke sometimes into a tornado of savage howls.

Cadieux watched the procession pass until it turned the bend of the river, all except the last canoe, in which, as he had expected, were two men – one an ordinary naked brave, the other a weird figure with a circular head-dress of feathers. His oiled bosom and shoulders were sprinkled with the under-down of an eagle's wing. This was the medicine man, the sorcerer, who always accompanied a war party. He sat in the stern and did the steering.

Cadieux's musket cracked, and a bullet went through the sorcerer's head. As he sank in death his paddle dropped and the canoe swung round athwart the current. The other Indian stopped paddling and half rose from his knees. The delay gave Cadieux time to reload, and a second bullet took the man in the throat. He tumbled overboard, and the current brought the canoe close to the near edge. In a second Cadieux was in the water, holding his musket high, and had scrambled aboard. He pitched the sorcerer into the stream, and the two bodies floated into a shallow, where the oil on their skins made a scum on the surface. Cadieux stuck the sorcerer's crown of feathers on his own head, seized a paddle and followed the others.

After that things became for Donald desperately exciting. Soon he saw the three canoes of the *coureurs de bois* approaching Calumet island, whose tall pines seemed to make a barrier across the river. The Iroquois, when they espied them, set up a demoniac shouting. Presently Donald saw the line of white water which marked the beginning of the rapids, and to which the Frenchmen boldly steered. The Indians drew into the left bank, where the portage began. They were far too engrossed with their purpose of slaughter to look back at their last canoe. In a few seconds they had beached their craft and set out on the portage trail. The game was in their hands, for from the trail they could command the canoes struggling in the rapids and at their leisure slaughter the crews.

Cadieux landed a little behind the rest and dived into the woods. He knew the place like his own hand, and was making for a point which commanded the portage. He made a wide circuit to avoid the Indians, while Donald held his breath... And then it seemed to the boy that the scene staged itself. There were the three canoes in the difficult rapids, following Poncet's lead, zigzagging to avoid sunken rocks, going slowly and cautiously except when it was necessary to risk a plunge of the current. There were the Indians, each man with his musket ready, now almost abreast of the canoes. And there was Cadieux, ahead of the Indians, ensconced above the path on a rock thatched with turf and gay with trilliums and the first wood lilies, scarcely breathing in spite of his hard race, his eyes merry and watchful, his finger on the trigger of his gun.

The track was narrow and could hold only one man at a time. An Iroquois came into view, a shot rang out, and he fell twenty feet into the rapids. Reloading took time, and the second Indian was ten paces nearer Cadieux before he met the same doom. A third followed; he did not fall into the stream but lay writhing in the path and tripped up the man who followed. This one too got his bullet, but the wound was not mortal, for he managed to glide like a snake into the thicket.

And then to Donald's amazement Cadieux began to sing, and his voice was so strong and rich that it seemed to be the singing not of one man but of a troop. His songs were strange things in that savage setting, for they told of faraway princesses and cavaliers of France, of shepherdesses of Touraine, of orange groves in Provence, of rose gardens in Navarre. One Donald knew well, for it was "Malbrouck s'en va t'en guerre", which he had learned in the nursery. It was eerie to hear those innocent old lays in that place of death.

The Iroquois checked. It looked as if they had stumbled into a hornets' nest and a troop of Frenchmen, deadly sharpshooters all, had come out to convoy the *coureurs de bois*. Cadieux fired again at a painted face, which drew back just in time, and followed his shot by shouting in different keys, as if many voices were joining in. The Iroquois had no love for fighting at a disadvantage and had deadly fear of a trap, since that was their own method of warfare. Moreover, they had lost their leader, whose body was now whirling down the rapids. There was a quick retreat, and soon the band were back in their canoes paddling furiously upstream.

All but one. Donald had seen a wounded Indian crawl into the covert. Suddenly the man revealed himself. As Cadieux rested on his musket, his ears strained to catch every sound, his spirits soared as he realised that the enemy was in flight. A rustle at his back made him turn, and he found his legs gripped by strong arms which pulled him to the ground. He grappled with his enemy, but his hands slipped on the oiled body, and an Iroquois knife was plunged deep in his side. The pain quickened his giant strength, his fingers found the Indian's throat, and a second later another carcase was in the river.

But Cadieux knew that he had won victory at the price of his life. The knife had gone deep, and the gush of blood told him that he had little time left on earth. He was moved to a strange exaltation. On the crest where he stood there was a little hollow caused by a fault in the rock. This should be his grave.

His strength was fast ebbing and he expended what remained like a miser. First with his axe he cut two branches, and with a piece of hemp from his pocket made a cross of them and set it up at the head of the grave. Then he cut green boughs and piled them at the edge. Then he stripped the bark from a white birch, and thereby made tablets on which, with the point of his knife, he could write his last testament.

He thought of his wife far away on the St Lawrence shore. He thought of his friends and his youth. He thought of his companions whose safety he had purchased with his blood. He thought of the bright world which he was leaving, and in which he had been happy. The poet awoke in him for the last time, and he made the death song of Cadieux which was to live in the hearts of his people.

He laid himself in the grave, and, while he sang the verses to a sad old tune, he wrote them on the birch bark. A raven fluttered down beside him, but flew away at the sound. A wolf looked over the edge and also fled.

> "*Petit rocher de la haute montagne,*"

he sang,

> "*Je viens ici finir cette campagne.*"

> "Little rock of the mountain side,
>   Here I rest from all my pride.
>   Sweet echo, hear my cry;
>   I lay me down to die."

He sang his last greetings to the birds and the woods, to his companions, to his wife and his children.

> "Say to my dear ones, nightingale,
>   My love for them can never fail.
>   My faith has known no stain,
>   But they see me not again."

And then, as his breath grew short, he pulled the coverlet of branches over him and wrote his last verse with a faltering hand.

"Now the world has dimmed its face,
Saviour of men I seek Thy grace.
Sweet Virgin ever blest,
Gather me to thy breast."

Twilight had fallen on the forest, and with the day went Cadieux.

Night passed, and next morning came three of the *coureurs* led by Du Gay, with a reserve of a dozen stout fellows from the settlement. They found everything quiet on the portage. The scouts they sent out reported that the night before the Iroquois had made their fires twenty miles to the west.

The rude cross showed them the grave of Cadieux. Donald saw them lift the body and carry it reverently to the settlement. Among the *coureurs de bois* many had died gallantly in faraway places, and no word had come of their end, but the story of Cadieux was there for all men to read. There was an old air which he had loved and which fitted the words inscribed on the birch bark, and the canoemen sang it like a funeral song when they brought the dead man to Montreal.

Donald wondered why his eyes were watering as if the sun had been too strong for them. He was puzzled, too, why he had seen no more fish in Baptiste's Pool, and why he felt so apathetic about next day's venture. Negog had stopped humming his queer tune and was looking for a match to relight his pipe.

Now Donald had no recollection of how he saw the pictures in the *Eau Dorée*, for that is the way of strong magic. But he remembered very clearly *what* he had seen and heard. So if you look at the book of *Chansons Populaires du Canada* which Father Laflamme has recently published, you will find two verses of Cadieux's song never before printed. The editor explains in a note that they were taken down from the recitation of a friend, and I do not mind telling you that that friend was Donald.

CHANSONS

What are the songs that Cadieux sings
Out in the woods when the axe-blade rings?
Whence the words and whence the tune
Which under the stars the boatmen croon?

Some are the games that children play
When they dance in rings on a noon in May,
And the maiden choir sings high and low
Under the blossomy orchard snow.
Some are the plaints of girls forlorn,
For lovers lost and pledges torn,
Told at eve to the evening star,
When the lit *tourelle* is a lamp afar.
Some are sung 'neath the dreaming trees
In modish garden pleasances,
Where a silken Colin indites his ode
To a shepherdess hooped and furbelowed,
And fat carp swim in the fountain's deep,
And the cares of the world have gone to sleep.
And some are the lays of the good green earth,
Of sunburnt toil and hobnailed mirth,
Where Time is loth to turn the page,
And lingers as in the Golden Age.
That is the tongue that Cadieux speaks
In his *bottes sauvages* and his leathern breeks –
Old sweet songs of the far-off lands,

Norman orchards and Breton sands,
Chicken-skin fans and high-heeled shoon, –
Squires and ladies under the moon, –
Which the night wind carries swift and keen
To the ears of wolf and wolverine,
And every beast in the forest's law, –
And maybe a prowling Iroquois.

CHAPTER 5

The Man Who Dreamed of Islands

Next day Donald got his salmon. It was in Baptiste's Pool, as he expected, and, though it was not very big – only eight pounds – it was his first, and he caught it on a nine-foot trout-rod.

It happened after tea, just in the way such things ought to happen. At the foot of the pool the Manitou gathered itself into a deep swirl, smooth as oil, which swept in a curve like a snake's back into a boulder-strewn shallow. On each side of the current there was a yard or two of slack water. Negog tied a rope to Donald's waist and the boy waded to the very edge of the swirl and just managed to get his fly into the slack beyond. There the salmon took him. It was mercifully inspired to go upstream, for it would have inevitably broken him among the boulders in the pool. He had a mighty tussle, and his line ran out to the last yard of backing. But after a breathless ten minutes the obliging fish, though still untired, came close to the near shore and was beautifully gaffed by Negog.

A first salmon is one of the highlights of life, and Donald missed nothing of its savour. He held it lovingly in his arms; he laid it on the turf and regarded it from different angles; hoarsely he demanded to know what it weighed. He was still too excited to have many words. Then Negog made a fire.

"We eat him," he said. "We have supper. I have brought salt and bread."

He cleaned the fish, cut two steaks from it, buttered the little pan which he carried in his bag, and set them to grill. The prospect of such a supper opened Donald's lips. He babbled.

"How many salmon has my father caught, Negog? Thousands – hundreds of thousands."

"I do not know. I think as many as the snowgeese in spring."

"You know that he caught the record fish in the Beauly."

"The Beauly! What is that?"

"A river in Scotland. Oh, a fine river, though not as big as the Manitou. I've seen it. I've been in Scotland. Once. I've seen the Scots hills. They're not covered with trees like ours, but bare and rocky, and some of them have sharp points. And I saw the Alps, too, and they're all snow and ice. The Rockies are like them. I want to go to the Rockies. Have you been there, Negog?"

The Indian shook his head. His attention was claimed by the salmon steaks which were beginning to frizzle nicely.

"Some day I'll go there," Donald went on in a high recitative, for he was a little above himself. "I'm going to climb the big bare mountains. My father says he gets tired of hills that cannot clear their feet of woods. And some day I'm going to catch a Scots salmon. They're very difficult, for they're not as plentiful as here, and there are no canoes, so you've got to cast a mighty long line. We're Scottish, you know. Our family were Jacobites, and had to clear out when Prince Charlie got beaten. We went to North Carolina, and had to clear out of there, too, when the Americans rebelled. We were something called Empire-loyals. Do you know what that means?"

Negog did not. He belonged to a Canada which knew nothing of the old frontier troubles.

"I had a great-great-great-great-uncle – I don't know how many 'greats.' He was a grand chap. His name was Alan Macdonnell. He came up from the United States and joined the fur traders. My father has found out a lot about him. He was always pushing farther West. He wanted to get to the high mountains and the sea."

The Indian raised his eyes from his cooking.

"Did he get there?" he asked.

"We can't tell. He never came back. My father says that he wishes he had the time to follow up his trail. When I'm a man I'm going to have a try at it. Maybe he was the first to get to the Pacific and nobody knows about it."

"That is well," said Negog. "It is right to follow the path of one's ancestors." But he spoke in Cree and Donald did not know what he was saying.

The boy surveyed the remains of his fish, now minus the steaks, with a regret that a thing so shapely should perish. Then he took up a flat stone and skimmed it over the river. It made five hops, which pleased him. The evening sun had turned Baptiste's Pool into a golden dazzle. The great central swirl was a mist of light, but the shallows at the edge were bright and clear. He saw something move in them which at first he thought was a fish. As he peered he saw that it was a picture.

Donald was looking at a place which he had never seen before, and yet which he seemed to know as intimately as Bellefleurs. He knew that he was in Scotland. The time was late afternoon. He was in a pass, between steep little hills red with heather. A stream had its source in a tiny well, and ran in a green strath between bogs to a beach of white sand. Beyond that was the sea, quiet as a mill-pond, a pale amber at the edge but a pool of gold where it caught the westering sun. In the middle distance lay a string of islands, low reefs except in the centre, where one rose to a ragged cockscomb of rock. The islands were deep blue like a sapphire, but the cockscomb was curiously gilded. To Donald it was more than a spectacle. He seemed to sniff a delectable odour of thyme and salt and peat, an odour he had never met before, and to have in his ears a continual calling of wild birds, plaintive and yet oddly comforting too. Somehow the place made him happy.

He had a sudden feeling that someone was beside him looking at the same prospect; so he swung round, but there was nothing but the bees and the birds and the tinkling stream. But he knew that someone had been there, and though he had not seen him, he knew what he looked like.

Then the picture faded, and he saw a big, dusty, raftered room, half office, half warehouse, in which two men were bending over a table of charts.

The pair wore breeches and full-skirted coats and small unpowdered wigs. They were both tall fellows, broad-shouldered, on the sunny side of middle age, with strong, harsh features; but one had a ruddy face, and the skin of the other was dark and sallow.

The dark man straightened himself and passed a hand over his forehead.

"I have a sore head, Sandy," he groaned, "and my eyes blink when I try to read Alan Macdonnell's cursed small maps. They are like a hen walking first in mud and then in snow. The Beaver Club madeira last night was a thought too potent. Faith, the Concern will have a braw year if our *voyageurs* covet the *Pays d'en Haut* as fast as we empty glasses to its prosperity."

The florid man laughed. "You were a bonny sight sitting on the floor at the Grand Voyage paddling like a fury with a pair of tongs. Man Sim, there was no shifting you. You said you were bound for Great Slave Lake and were running the Rapids of the Drowned. You got that from nephew Alan? Well, sore head or no, we must settle Alan's business today. The man's my own blood relation, but he's as uncomfortable a body in the service as a catfish in a shoal of herrings. When I pressed the Concern to take him I thought he would settle down to be a decent bourgeois, as keen on his profits as the rest of them. Deil a chance! He doesn't care a docken for the siller, and he's as restless as a flea in a blanket. We tried him on the Churchill and he was away over the Portage la Loche to the Athabasca. We tried him on the Athabasca and the next heard of him was on the Peace. We tried him at Peace Point, and bless my soul if he doesn't disappear for eighteen months, and bring back nothing but these scarts of the pen he calls his maps. An unprofitable servant, Sim, I say, though he's my own sister's son."

The man called Sim shook his head. "We'll never make a trader of him, but I'm not so sure we may not make something better. He's the kind of dog that finds game, even if he leaves it to others to bring back. And faith, Sandy! the Concern needs that kind of dog. There's the Hudson's Bay gentry keen to push us off the Saskatchewan, and the X. Y. lads driving us back from the north, and the Americans poaching our ground in the south. We've a mighty need for new territory, and your Alan may be the one to find it."

"You've talked with him? What's his notion?"

"He's for crossing the mountains. He's seen them from a hundred miles off, and they've affected his brain. You know how far ben he is with the tribes. He's lived with them and talked with them – all the outland folk, like the Beavers and the Piegans and the Slaves, and queerer ones still at the very ends of the earth. Well, he's heard tell from them of roads through the mountains, and of lands beyond them fair hotching with beaver and marten and maybe new kinds of fur not hitherto heard tell of. At the end is the sea and the coast, which the Spaniards claim. In that his story is correct, for I've word from home that my Lords of the Admiralty have got their eye on that quarter."

"Whereabouts does he want to cross the mountains?"

"He's changed his view. First he had a notion that the easiest route was up the Peace river; but further enquiries made him less certain of it. Then he was for a place far up in the north in the Slave country called the River of the Mountains.* But now he has a new plan. His road is the Athabasca, for he has heard there's an easy pass to the west. That's not our information, for we've been told that the Athabasca high up is nothing but a fearsome torrent in which no canoe can live, and that it comes

---

* This, I think, must have been the Liard.

out of a muckle mountain of ice. But he's besotted on the idea, and nothing will shake him."

"The man's mad, though I say it that shouldn't," said the other. "Aye been. The Macdonnells are as daft as a yett in a high wind. You know about his forebears? They were close kin to Clanranald, and after Culloden had to shift out of Scotland to save their necks. Wild Jacobites, every one of them. They settled in the Carolinas, and Alan's grandfather made himself a comfortable little property. But Alan's father had the daft strain in his blood. He went west to the Mississippi and never came back, and when the war began nothing would content Alan but to fight on the side of the British and lose every stick and stone he possessed. He and his black servant Hector came for refuge to Canada and the rest you ken."

The sallow man gathered the charts into a bundle. "Mad or no," he said, "I'm for using him. I propose we send him with the new Brigade and post him at the west end of the Saskatchewan. We'll give him Davie Murchison as his assistant to attend to business, and if he has a notion to take a look at the mountains we'll turn a blind eye. The pointer dog may find us game. What do you say to having him in? He's waiting in the Deputy-Commissioner's room. Lord! lord! but I have a sore head!"

The man who answered the summons was half a foot shorter than the two chiefs of the Nor'West Company and a decade younger – little more than thirty, perhaps, though the deep lines of his face and the network round his eyes told of a hard youth. He wore his own hair, which was black as a sloe, and his clothes, since he was for the time a city dweller, were of the latest fashion which Montreal could provide. In particular he had a scarlet waistcoat edged with silver lace. But his lean body, with no ounce of unnecessary flesh, the beaten bronze of his complexion, and the smouldering fire in his eyes gave the lie to his finery. Here was one who was happier in the wilds than on a city pavement. His two superiors were hard, active fellows, but compared to him they looked soft and lethargic.

Donald knew that this was great-uncle Alan. He knew also that this was the man who had been behind him when he looked out on the Scots islands. The voice was familiar, but how he could not tell. It had a soft Highland lilt in it, and now and then Alan would slip into the Gaelic and be answered by one or the other in the same tongue.

It was a friendly talk, more like a gossip of equals than the instructions of master to servant. Throughout there was the courtesy of the Gael. Alan was to go with the Brigade to the North Saskatchewan, and at a certain point on its head waters, in the foothills of the mountains, to complete a new fort of which the foundations had been laid the year before. It would be known as Knoydart House, out of compliment to its maker.

"Keep your eye on the Bay men," he was told. They have a place on the Red Deer, a score of miles off, and there's word that they purpose to set up another for the Blackfoot trade still nearer you. But at that job our *voyageurs* should beat their clumsy Orkneymen... You will finish the fort before the winter and have the dark months to look round you for trade next spring..." The sallow man stopped, and there was a suspicion of a twinkle in his eye.

Alan saw it and laughed. He understood what it meant.

"I will do your bidding, sirs," he said. "Next spring I'll continue to look round, and by God's grace extend the circuit of my observations. Some day I may have a fine story for your ears."

After this the pictures came fast, and Donald held his breath as he watched the details of Montreal's annual venture into the wilderness. He saw each stage in the progress of the Brigade: the procession of carts which carried the stuff past the Lachine rapids; the big canoes and the bateaux which bore goods and men up the St. Lawrence and through the great lakes and over the portages at Niagara and Sault St Marie, till Thunder Bay was reached and the start of the route to the north. There Alan Macdonnell and his party changed into the light northern canoes, and by way of Rainy Lake and the Lake of the Woods came to Lake Winnipeg. After that they went north to where the Saskatchewan entered that lake, and then, with many portages, up that noble river past stations of the Bay men and of the Nor'-Westers, past the big fork where the southern branch came in – endless days in the deep trench of the river bed, till the banks grew shallower, and over the poplar scrub rose the green ridges of the foothills.

Donald saw the *voyageurs* reel off the miles with their tireless paddling – a stroke a second and twelve hours' work in the day. The canoemen were not the *mangeurs de lard* – the pork eaters of the St Lawrence; but folk who summered and wintered in the wilds and knew every trick of white water. They were a small race – otherwise they could not have fitted into the canoes – lean, short-legged, but with brawny arms and enormous shoulders; each had his nickname, and one of surpassing ugliness, whose face had been slapped by a bear, was known as "Pretty Maid". A merry race, too, who never stopped singing while they toiled, and at night in camp when they had finished supper made the woods ring with their glees. There was music all the way, for Hector, Alan's black servant, was a piper, and when they approached a fort would play a sprig to announce their advent – not "The Campbells are Coming", which the Bay men affected, but some quick-step of the honest clans.

They came to Knoydart House in a warm September afternoon, and were welcomed by Davie Murchison, who had been holding the fort all summer. Then, before the snows began, there was a busy season. The ground had been already cleared and a stockade built, and the task now was to erect storehouse and dwelling-house and quarters for the men. The *voyageurs* were expert at the job; the logs from the woods were so grooved that they needed no nails to keep them in position. The interiors were lined with a white clay which made an excellent plaster, floors were levelled, windows were glazed with oiled deerskin, great chimneys and hearths were built, in which an ox could have been roasted. Last of all, a tall pine was set up and the flag of the Nor'-West broken from the pole, while Hector blew manfully on his pipes.

Then it seemed to Donald that he saw winter settle down on the fort. Though the Bay had posts very near, the rivalry was not serious, for the *voyageurs* knew better the ways of the people and the land than the raw Orkneymen. The Nor'-West packed its goods in light bales with waterproof coverings, while the Bay had theirs in clumsy great casks wrapped in rotten canvas, so that they had always to be opening and drying their stuff. The Orkneymen had not the Frenchmen's extra sense for difficult water. More, they were not so close to the Indian mind. They might do well enough with the Crees of the Churchill swamps and with the Blood and Blackfoot clans of the prairies, but in the foothills they were in a strange land. Alan had a light hand with the *voyageurs* and was well served. Sometimes he used to curse them in Latin, a speech which they respected as the only tongue which the Devil could not understand.

It was an open winter, for the chinook wind came often to raise the temperature and melt the snow. With the New Year, Alan, having finished his main task, handed over to Davie Murchison and began to explore the countryside. He and Hector moved on snowshoes, and food and bedding were carried on sledges drawn by a team of dogs, which they drove fanwise and not in the tandem fashion of the eastern forests. He visited the hunting camps of the Piegans, tucked into the crannies of the foothills, and bought from them deer meat and bear meat and buffalo meat for the fort. And always, wherever he went, he talked to the Indians of the passes in the mountains, especially of one pass that led straight to the setting sun. He had long had news of it – the *voyageurs* called it the Tête Jaune – and now he could plan the road to it. It was to be reached not by the Saskatchewan, his own river, but by the far northern Athabasca. His travels took him close up to the knees of the mountains, and one blue day he saw in a great semi-circle the white peaks which

71

crowded about the Tête Jaune. On that occasion Hector caught up his pipes and played "The Faraway Hills".

On the first day of April Alan said goodbye to Knoydart House. He gave Davie Murchison instructions about getting off the Knoydart contingent of the east-going Brigade for the grand rendezvous at Thunder Bay. "I will send back word if I get a chance," he said, "and will myself return, if God permits, before the winter."

He took Hector with him and four Piegans, one of whom had crossed the mountains and knew something of the language of the mountain tribes. Three of the *voyageurs* were to accompany the party to the divide, to take back the dog teams which would be useless in the upper glens.

They set out in bleak weather, the last snow flurries of winter, and now for the first time Donald could study Alan's face. Funnily enough he seemed to have known it all his life. It was a young face, much battered by weather, with dancing brown eyes, like the eddies in a peat stream, and a mouth which, though stern in repose, had a laugh lurking at its corners. This was the kind of man Donald felt that he would choose above all others to go travelling with.

The snow was deep and firm until they were inside the white fangs of the hills. A broad strath took them to the summit of the Tête Jaune, beyond which the waters ran southward or westward. Thence the dogs were sent back to Knoydart House, but one of the *voyageurs*, Pierre Laframboise, begged that he might continue the journey, having a wish, he said, to see what happened to the setting sun.

They made a lobstick at the head of the pass by trimming a fir until its topmost branches were bunched like a toadstool – this as a landmark and a memorial. Then Alan and Hector and Pierre and the four Piegans back-packed their stores, and started to blaze a trail to the west. It was a slow and toilsome job, for spring came on them like a thunderclap. The snow melted into mud, the hillsides dissolved into water, and every stream was a torrent.

Alan was a martinet, and would suffer no deviation from the western route, though the trend of the waters was to the southward. There was much weary climbing of lateral ridges, sometimes by deer path, sometimes by Indian trail, most often by a track hewn through a virgin jungle. The larches were greening and the spring flowers had made a bright carpet in the upland meadows when at last they came to a valley with a strong river flowing honestly westward. That night Hector's pipes played "The Glen is Mine".

The time was over for back-packing, and boats must be built. This was a job for the Piegans. There was no birch of any size to be had, so the craft must be made not of bark but of skins. Alan shot the needed number of bull moose, and the hides were cunningly prepared by Pierre. The frames of the two canoes were of cedar, as were the paddles, the skins were sewn together with cords made from the roots of spruce, and the caulking was done with melted pine-gum. Pierre, who had his countrymen's eye for colour, managed to manufacture a paint from certain roots and leaves, and decorated the high prows with red, white, and green. The work meant a fortnight's delay, during which Alan went hunting to replenish the camp larder. Pemmican was made by Pierre, good pemmican, for it was rich in fat and plentifully sprinkled with berries.

Summer was now upon them, and to Donald's eyes the little party, as it descended the broad stream, which somehow he knew to be the Fraser, seemed to be creeping daily into a land of richer greenery and brighter sunshine. Winter clothes were shed, and in the daytime they were half-naked, though in the evening the ravenous flies forced them again into their garments. They found human occupants in the land – Carrier tribes, who were friendly enough and who conversed with the Piegan who had a smattering of their speech. They were not a far-travelled folk and knew little of the land beyond their tribal bounds; but they had heard of the Great Bitter Water; this river ran into it, they said, but after a violent course, which one of them described by flinging himself on the ground and kicking his heels in the air. This warning was not what decided Alan. He was like a man following an oracle, for nothing would content him but a straight road to the west. So when they came to the point where the Fraser swung to the south, he left it unhesitatingly and directed the canoes up an east-running tributary. He would not deviate one mile from his path into the sunset.

They were in the heats of summer, heats broken by violent thunder-storms and occasional days of mist and drizzle. So far good fortune had attended them, but now their luck changed. They were in a country of small streams linking up big lakes, and that meant long portages. Their first disaster was that the Piegans left them. The Babine Indians, whose country they were now traversing, were a peaceable race, ready to help the travellers; but it would have been better had they been warlike and menacing. The Piegan who spoke the mountain tongues was their undoing. For the Indians of the plains have not the magic of the hills and they fear what they do not know. The Babines told them tales of warlocks and witches and of vampires and werewolves and ravening animal spirits which turned their joints into water. There came a day when they announced that they could go no farther into this ill-omened land, a land of bottomless mires, and moss-hung forests, and mountains which crumbled. There was no dissuading them. Alan wrote a letter to Davie Murchison giving him news of the journey, but it was never delivered, for the Piegans, being unused to white water, perished in one of the Fraser rapids.

This was bad, but worse was the death of Pierre the *voyageur*. There came a week of heart-breaking toil, when the company, lacking the stalwart Piegans, whose loss was ill supplied by the dwarfish Babines, struggled over the last divide to the Skeena and the Pacific. There were long portages through forests full of tall decayed timber, where it took an hour for the axes to hew a yard of trail. Maddened by flies, sick with fatigue, choking with the miasma of the rotting woodlands, the party had all but reached their goal, an inky black lake which emptied towards the new watershed. Then suddenly out of the air came death. A fallen tree had been caught in a crotch of a neighbour and the passage of the men shook it loose, so that it crashed upon their rear, breaking Pierre's back like a dry twig. The stern of one of the boats was also damaged, and it took Alan three days' labour to mend it.

One boat was cached by the lake shore, and the other, containing Alan, Hector, and four of the Babines, began the long descent to the Pacific. It was now early autumn, and in that country where there were no maples, the woods became a delicate harmony in yellow – orange and saffron and gold… Donald observed a change in his kinsman's looks. The labours of the last portages had taken heavy toll of his strength, and he had become very lean and grey in the face. Food he scarcely touched, and he spoke little, except to give orders. No more snatches of song, with which he had once cheered the road, and when Hector would have got out his pipes a frown forbade him. The man seemed to be in a fever, eager to be on the move and in terror lest he should be impeded. He might have been a fugitive with the avenger of blood behind him.

Forest creeks gave place to hill streams as they slipped from the tableland to the sea. Presently they were in the jaws of the Coast mountains, a strait funnel between peaks which ran up to eternal snows. Their Babine guides at night brought some of the Tsimshian Indians to their bivouac, and since Alan had a few words of the Babine tongue he could ask questions. But he had only one. How far were they from the Great Bitter Water? How near to the Ultimate Islands? Mostly he got shaken heads for a reply, but one man apparently understood him, and with a stick drew a plan on the shore gravel.

Then one morning they reached the sea tides. Alan tasted the water and a new light came into his wild eyes. He bade Hector take up his pipes and play "The White Sands of Barra".

It was plain that Alan was very ill. Hector had to lift him ashore in the evening; he ate little food, but suffered from a raging thirst; he had begun to talk with himself, and babbled often like a man in a nightmare. To the Indians he seemed "fey," – one on whom the hand of God had been laid, and they hastened to obey his lightest word... And then one flaming evening the fiord opened into an ocean bay, and the sun set in crimson beyond a horizon of sea. Faintly outlined against the crimson were the shadows of far mountains.

Alan was on his feet peering into the west. Now at last the fever seemed to have left his eyes.

"Rejoice!" he cried, "*Chunnaic mi m'eileanan,*" and Hector knew his meaning. That night on his pipes he played without reproof that lilt of triumph, "A Kiss of the King's Hand".

Next morning the dying man embarked in one of the big dug-outs used for the ocean journey. There were Haidas there from the Islands, come to barter sea-otter skins for candle-fish oil, and such was the spell cast by Alan that they readily gave him a passage. With a sad heart Donald watched that strange ferrying. Behind were the snow peaks of the Coast range, and the thousand mountain miles which separated Alan from the white folk. In front over the gleaming morning sea rose the tall woods and the green muffled hills of the Ultimate Islands.

"I will die there," said Alan. "That is the fate I have always sought, for it was the fortune spae'd for me as a laddie. You, Hector, will see that there is a stone with the proper writing set over my grave, and you will go home somehow and some time and tell my friends what befell me. Tell them that I have reached the goal of all my dreams. I would have written it, but I have no paper, and I am too near death."

He died soon after he was brought ashore. A group of Haidas, tall men with the raven totem on their foreheads, were there to greet him, and their medicine man made a great lamenting over him, while Hector played that most heart-rending of all airs, "Macruimen's Farewell"... Then it seemed to Donald that a great slab of black slate was laid over the grave, and under Hector's direction words were engraved thereon. They were *Chunnaic mi m'eileanan fhein* – "I have seen my islands". The date was added.

The picture dissolved and two others succeeded. One showed Hector's doings – how in a Haida boat he sailed south, was captured by a Spanish man o' war, taken to Panama, and finally, after many adventures, reached Canada by sea. He never saw Montreal and the headquarters of the Nor'-Westers, for he died of phthisis at Halifax, so Alan's message was undelivered. The other was a picture of Alan's grave. A group of English seamen stood around it, among them a square-faced sturdy man, who was Captain George Vancouver. He was reading the inscription aloud and making havoc of the Gaelic.

"There's been an Englishman here before," he said. "That date's in good English. But God knows what the rest of the lingo is. It looks like a lunatic who had a cold in his head."

"Hullo!" said Donald's father one evening when he was reading his three-day-old newspaper. "They've found an inscription in Gaelic in the Queen Charlotte Islands. Dated, too. There must be a queer story behind that."

"It was great-uncle Alan," said Donald.

His father laughed. "Perhaps it was. If we could prove that, then Alan Macdonnell reached the Pacific from Canada four years before Alexander Mackenzie."

THE BLESSED ISLES

The air is quiet as a grave,
   With never a wandering breeze
Or the fall of a breaking wave
   In the hollow shell of the seas.
Ocean and heavens are a maze
   Of hues like a peacock's breast,
And far in the rainbow haze
   Lie the Isles of the West.

Uist and Barta and Lews –
   Honey-sweet are the words –
They set my heart in a muse
   And give me wings like a bird's.
Darlings, soon will I fly
   To the home of the tern and the bee,
And deep in the heather lie
   Of the Isles of the Sea.

But they say there are other lands
   For him who has heart and will,
Whiter than Barra's sands,
   Greener than Icolmkill,
Where the cool sweet waters flow,
   And the White Bird sings in the skies
Such songs as immortals know
   In the fields of Paradise.

So I'll launch my boat on the seas
    And sail o'er the shadowy deep,
Past the Island of Apple Trees
    And the little Island of Sheep,
And follow St Brandan's way
    Far into the golden West,
Till I harbour at close of day
    In the Isles of the Blest.

CHAPTER 6

Big Dog

It promised to be a hot day, but the light south wind blowing in from the Gulf had still a morning freshness as Donald pranced down the slope between the camp and the river. He had no plans except a desire to see Negog and to find out what Aristide Martel was doing. If Joe Petit-Pont was stacking hay it might be good fun to give him a hand. Or they might take the dog Glooskap (he had come from Nova Scotia as a puppy and had got his name there) and go into the woods and watch him chase the squirrels. Glooskap was getting fat and was as likely to catch a squirrel as a wild duck; but hope sprang eternal in his breast, and he was a comic figure as he lay sprawled at the foot of a sugar maple while his quarry spat at him from above.

Or there were the river and the canoes. They might go exploring up to the foot of the waterfall.

Simone Martel waved to him from the road which led from the village. She had become very lady-like since she had gone to school, and the new dignity made her slower in the race, though once she had been the fastest runner of them all. Also she now wore a neat straw hat, and her hair, once like a bramble bush for confusion, was tidily plaited.

"Jimmy Brush is here," she announced.

Donald shouted and then whistled long.

"Where is he?" he demanded.

"He's with Aristide, and they're at Cold Waters."

"Come on," said Donald, "I'll race you there."

"I can't come yet," said Simone primly. "I go to see my aunt Anastasie, who has a migraine, and then – "

But Donald was already halfway across the big pasture, jumping the little seedling firs, and howling like a dervish.

Jimmy Brush was to Donald and Aristide what Huckleberry Finn was to Tom Sawyer, the perfect boy, and his life was the fulfilment of their wildest dreams. He never went near a school or a church, and social duties weighed on him not at all; but he was profoundly learned in more important matters than Latin and arithmetic, and he had the fine manners which are due to perfect health, imperturbable good humour, and a heavy-handed parent. His age was pretty much Donald's, but life had already begun to write on his face, and he looked older. The profession of his father was a mystery, but handyman was perhaps the best description, since there were few things he could not turn his hand to. The Brushes were genuine nomads, for father and son travelled all the roads of Quebec and Gaspé in a kind of springless buggy drawn by an ancient horse. April released them from some lair in the cities, and until the first snows their wayside fires crackled by night in the lee of the pine woods or among the gravel of the river shore.

Jimmy's mother had been Irish, and his father claimed mysteriously to be French, and had a long story of a Brouche who had been a great man up Lac St Jean way. But his real origin was proclaimed by his high cheekbones and russet skin, and dark, deep-set eyes – all of which Jimmy faithfully reproduced. The Brushes were of Indian race, though they never talked about it, and appeared to speak no Indian tongue. They were not Crees, or Montagnais, or Hurons, or any of the eastern or northern stocks. Father Laflamme knew all about them, and so did Negog, who was always respectful when he spoke of them. They were Plains Indians from the very distant west – Bloods or Blackfoot or Stonies or Piegans – and they showed their origin in one curious way. They had learned woodcraft in the east, but they had horsecraft in their bones. There was no horse ailment that the elder Brush could not doctor, and Jimmy would talk to Celestin Martel's percherons as to old friends, and get answers out of them.

Donald found the two boys at Cold Waters, which was a cleft in the hillside with an icy spring in it. There the Brush tent was pitched; before it were the smouldering ashes of the breakfast fire, the elder Brush busy with a new halter, Aristide prone on his face, an eager audience for Jimmy, who was speaking in his slow, quiet French. An Indian tent is apt in summer to smell strong, but not so the Brushes', for the flaps were tied back and the bedding was being aired like a badger's straw.

Jimmy could not budge until the evening, for he had moccasins to shape for his stay in Bellefleurs, having just completed the ruin of a pair of Quebec shoes.

"Negog told me Jimmy had come," Aristide informed Donald. "He wants us to be down by the river tonight before sundown. Bad luck I can't come, for they're stacking the hay to-day and we'll work till it's dark. It will be all right tomorrow, and Jimmy will have finished his job then."

Donald spent a pleasant day in the company of Joe Petit-Pont and the Martel family, and returned to tea with his hair full of hayseed and a most superior thirst. Thereafter he found Negog sorting nets on the camp verandah, and squatted beside him. Negog was in one of his silent moods, and Donald was glad when Jimmy Brush appeared as quietly as the fall of a leaf. Jimmy had a half of his blood white, which, blended with his Indian ancestry, gave him the figure of a lean, dusky young Apollo. His slim legs showed that he was no woodsman, for the snowshoe muscles were undeveloped, and, unlike the forest-bred, he was straight as an arrow. He spoke fluent French, and the slangy English of the cities, and he had a smattering of half a dozen Indian dialects. His smile, Donald's mother used to say, was the most engaging thing on the continent.

Having been to the Toronto races that spring he babbled about horses, a subject which did not greatly interest Donald. Negog listened attentively and sniffed. Then he said something in a strange tongue, which Jimmy seemed to recognise, for he laughed.

"This guy says horses are only big dogs," he told Donald. "He says I got to wise up about my family, for they were about sunk by the big dogs until they got their guns. I sure will ask Dad about it."

"He doesn't know," said Negog grimly.

"That's just too bad."

Jimmy was on his feet and racing Donald to the river before Negog had tidied up his nets and put them away.

Donald's feet were drawn by some instinct to the edge of the shingle, and the low-pitched talk of Negog and Jimmy and even the murmur of the stream, were muted in the twilit stillness. Of his senses only his eyes were awake, and in the molten gold of the shallows a picture shaped itself...

He saw a great flat country, wider and wilder than any he had ever known. Midway in a deep trench a muddy river looped and twined, which he knew to be the South Saskatchewan. Nothing obstructed the vision until it reached the horizon, which was the extreme limit of sight like a horizon at sea; but towards the west the hawk eyes of the Indians could discern a shadowy sierra of blue mountain. But, though as a whole the land was flat, it was less a plain than a hummocky plateau, for it rolled and eddied in smooth waves of downland. It was early summer, and the pasture, still untouched by the plough, was fresh and juicy, though except for the great river there was no running water.

An Indian tribe were shifting camp. The tall painted teepees were coming down, and the tent poles were being fastened to the backs of the dogs, so that they formed a travois supporting big skin packs which trailed like a sledge. There was a terrific bustle at the rear of the camp where the squaws and children were collected, but there was quiet in the front, where the warriors were formed up in their societies. These Piegans were tall folk, like all of the Blackfoot confederacy, slim, long of leg, and light on their feet as antelopes.

Donald's attention was fixed on one of the youngest of the warriors, a boy not out of his teens. He was that ancestor of more than two centuries ago to whom Jimmy Brush had cast back, for, though older and more fully developed, he was Jimmy's living image. Donald found that he knew all about him, what he had done and was going to do, and that in some queer way he could see inside his mind.

The boy's old name had been Two Dogs, because two dogs had been the first sight that his mother had seen after his birth. But now he had a new name, for at the buffalo hunt three days ago he had been solemnly admitted into the best of the tribal societies, the Thunder Hawks, and he had been given the new name of West Wind. More, the Sun Dance of yesterday, when offerings had been made to the Great Spirit and there had been the ritual of the cutting of buffalo tongues by the women, had been in honour of his own mother, the most famous lady of the tribe. She had been given a wonderful medicine bag of raw hide, full of precious ceremonial things, and West Wind, as her eldest son, had had another. It was his dearest possession and was now packed on a dog's back in the special care of his blood brother Grey Wolflet, who had hurt his leg at the buffalo hunt and so was not equal to battle.

For it was to battle that they went. Gone were the gaudy blues and greens and yellows of the Sun Dance, and the braves were painted with the sombre Spanish brown which meant war. Their arrows and spears were new-tipped with obsidian, for a party of young men had just been to the mountains in the far south to get supplies of that precious stone.

War had been in the air ever since the buffalo hunt. The Piegans claimed as their hunting ground all the land drained by the southern feeders of the South Saskatchewan, between what are now called the Old Man and the Red Deer rivers, that being their share of the Blackfoot territory. But at the buffalo hunt there had been few buffalo, since others had been there before them, and the hollows were raw with the blood and bones of beasts newly killed. In the evening when the hunters turned back, the smoke of camp fires was seen in the west, and word was brought that the Snake tribe were hunting there – were indeed moving eastward into the sacred Piegan preserves.

It was a challenge that must be met. A council of the elders had decreed that these interlopers from the south should be summarily punished and that the tribe was capable of dealing with them without help from Blood or Blackfoot... West Wind shook his new spear in the air, and lovingly felt the points of his new-tipped arrows. Soon they would be finding a home in Snake parts.

To Donald's excited eyes the fight seemed a muddled affair. The Piegans advanced on a broad front, like beaters at a partridge drive, with their old men, their sick, women, children, and baggage dogs sheltering behind them. There were no rearguards or flank guards. The Snakes, short, broad, sinewy fellows painted with stripes of green and red, were notably fewer in numbers than the Piegans, but they had horses, a score at least, wild, leggy beasts with yard-long manes. Their tactics were simple and effective. They spread out before the Piegan advance and, while their centre slowly retreated, the horsemen on the wings got to the Piegan rear and scuppered the camp followers.

The inevitable result followed. The Piegans turned to protect their belongings and then the Snake centre attacked. There was no great slaughter, for the Piegans, being more numerous, were able to encircle their baggage train, and the horsemen had no longer a chance. But they were compelled to fall back, and only nightfall stopped the running fight. Women and children had been murdered and much plunder taken. West Wind's mother had an arrow wound in her arm, and his companion-in-arms, Grey Wolflet, had been slain and scalped.

In the darkness of the night, when the pickets had reported that the enemy had retired, the Piegan warriors held solemn counsel.

First the old men spoke. The Great Spirit, they said, had favoured their enemies, and had given them Big Dogs that could carry a man and run swift as the wind. It was foolish to contend against the Great Spirit. These Dogs from the south were no doubt endowed with magic, not only with speed but with immortality. No Piegan could bend a bow against them, therefore let them take counsel with others of the Blackfoot confederacy, and make a treaty with the Snake people to share their hunting ground.

But the view of the elders was not that of the younger braves. They would have none of this treaty-making. The Big Dogs (*Misstutim* they called them) were doubtless animals and like other dogs. They were from the south, and it was well known that the south was the home of strange beasts – serpents that rattled, and such like. Who said they were immortal? None had died in the fight because the Piegans had been too confused to shoot at them. At the next encounter let them see whether the brutes were arrow-proof.

The discussion raged. The old men stuck to their view and the young men to theirs. It was pointed out that the Big Dogs might be mortal, but that they ran so fast that it would be hard to hit them.

"Not faster than an elk," said West Wind, "and elk have often fallen to our bows."

They might be hit, said the elders, but an arrow at long range would not cripple them, and the shots could only be at long range since in an instant the beasts were in their ranks.

"Then let us hold our fire," said West Wind.

But if we do that, the old men argued, the Dogs will still overtake us, for it is well known that arrows, though they may eventually kill, have no instant stopping power.

Then West Wind spoke. He was listened to, for he was the son of his mother, and the heart of the tribe had gone out to him since that day he had lost Grey Wolflet, his blood brother.

"The Big Dogs are a deadly peril," he said. "I have seen them and I fear them. Some day the Snakes will come with many hundreds of them, and then the Piegan people will perish from the earth. It is also true what my fathers say, that our arrows, though sped from stout bows by strong arms, will not halt their charge in time. That much is agreed. But it is wrong to speak of making truce with the Snakes and sharing our hunting-grounds, for the Snakes are a greedy folk and will not be content until they have eaten us up."

He stopped for a moment and all eyes were turned on him.

"I put to you another plan," he said. "It is rumoured that our cousins, the Assiniboine people, have got a new weapon, a stick which speaks loud and kills from far off. I have spoken with those who have seen it. They got it from the Crees of the Plains who live in the north by this river of ours, and the Crees in turn got it from the white men with hair on their chins, of whom we have heard. Now hearken to my plan. Our cousins the Assiniboines will not give us the sticks, for they have few. The white hairy men, who have many, live far off, we know not where. But let us go to the Crees of the Plains, who have more than the Assiniboines, and who, it appears, will sell."

"How will you pay?" he was asked.

"Not with skins and wampum," was the answer, "but with a medicine bundle, for this is strong magic."

"And who will bargain?"

"If it is permitted, I will go myself," said West Wind.

He took his mother's medicine bundle, the gift of the tribe at the Sun Dance, for it contained treasures which all Indian peoples prized. There were pipes made of stone from the Sacred Quarry in Minnesota; there was a black beaver skin; there was an antelope's prong horns curiously bound together; and the skins of bright-coloured birds from the south; and queer nuts from the mountains which were the provender for the dead on their journey to the Country of Souls. Most precious of all there was a fragment of thunder-stone which all the world knew made its owner the special charge of the Great Spirit.

With the medicine bundle slung on his back beside his bow, and his quiver and tomahawk at his belt, West Wind set out on his journey. He went north by east, following the great river, and Donald could trace every stage. Each night his tiny fire crackled in a nook of hill where he roasted duck or goose or hare. Each day his long loping stride carried him farther out of the Blackfoot land into the tree country. First there were bluffs of poplar and maple and willow by the streams; then bigger woods in what is now called the park country, and then, when his river had become a mighty flood, there came forests of pointed trees which thickened into a dark cloud in the north.

There he met the first Cree bands and smoked a pipe with them. They received him well, for the war paint was gone from his face, save for the yellow rings on his cheeks which betokened a messenger, and in any case his mien was friendly and his address both dignified and gracious. He was led to the principal camp of the nation by the side of a lake so big that the eye, looking across it, could see no land. There, after he had eaten, he spoke with shamans and sachems in the centre of the ring of warriors.

He told the story of the Snakes and the Big Dogs, and he told it so that he was believed.

"What have you come here for?" the Cree chief asked. "To seek an alliance?"

"Not so," said West Wind. "The Cree people and the Piegan people live too far apart to be allies though they may well be friends. I come to exchange medicine bags."

Then followed a long chaffering. Each article in West Wind's bag had attached to it some special incantation, for ritual things are of no use unless the spirit be attuned to them. Such incantations West Wind had to expound. The bag was strong magic and the Crees coveted it for their tribe.

"What is the price?" they asked.

"Another medicine bag," was the answer. "And in it must be some of the sticks which the white men have given you and which you sold to our cousins the Assiniboines."

He asked for eight muskets, and after a long argument he was given six with the requisite powder and shot.

West Wind had scarcely rejoined his tribe with his new medicine bag when the Snakes struck again. They did not wait for the Piegans to drive them out of their hunting grounds, but swept eastward into lands which had been Piegan since time immemorial. It was a raid and not a fight and it fell at night in the third quarter of the moon. A band of twenty mounted men dashed upon the sleeping camp, slaughtered and scalped, and disappeared like a morning mist.

Four days later the Piegans marched westward to the battle which would decide for good and all the fate of their nation. West Wind was by the side of the War Chief, and with him were six young men, their faces curiously painted in brown with splashes of black around and above the eyes. These were the lords of the muskets. There was no ammunition to spare, so they could not practise shooting, but West Wind had been told the way of it by the Plains Crees, and he laboured to instruct his men. The sticks must be held stiff, and when the triggers were pulled there must not be the throw forward of the bow. If it were possible, a man should shoot lying prone, with the stick resting on a stone or tuft, but at all costs the eye must run straight along the stick to the point which was the enemy's breast.

"We are new to this task," he told the War Chief. "We must draw close to the Snakes, risking their arrows until we are not fifty yards apart. Then each stick will speak with certainty. My counsel is that after they have spoken twice the whole Piegan line should charge, for the Snakes will have the fear of the sticks in their heart and will assuredly run."

It came about as West Wind foresaw. The enemy were discovered in a bend of the Saskatchewan, full fed, for they had just made a great slaughter of buffaloes. The Piegans had the good luck to find a position where their flanks were protected by the river and a knob of hill, so that the horsemen could not get at their rear except by a long circuit.

The Piegan braves advanced steadily till they were well within arrow range without firing a shot, and the Snake bowmen took heavy toll of them. Two of West Wind's musketeers were crippled and their places were taken by others from the reserve. Then at fifty paces the Snakes, about to be unleashed in a final charge, had a staggering experience. Six of the first-rank Piegans dropped on their knees or on their bellies, there was a noise like little thunder-claps, and something spat out into their midst. Men fell dead with no projecting spear or arrow to show how death had found them.

The Snake ranks wavered. Three bold youths sprang forward, and again came the spitting. And then the Piegans raised their war shout and dashed upon the wonderstruck and terrified Snakes. The spitting death came again, and also a flight of arrows, and soon the Snake people were fleeing through the river shallows, reddening the water with their blood. The horsemen led the flight, all save one whose mount was killed under him, and he was trampled to death in the press.

That night there was a great feasting. West Wind had his forehead painted with the mystic mark of the Piegans, the loop and the crossed arrows, in bright orange on a red ochre background. Word came that one of the Big Dogs had been killed, and the Piegan braves went down to look at it.

"No dog," said West Wind. "It is a deer without horns."

But as he gazed at it and noted the small clean head, the lean powerful flanks and shoulders, the delicate feet, a new feeling woke in him. This beast was a portent and a marvel, but it might also be a delight... Some day, he thought, when there was peace between the peoples, he would take a trip to the south and visit the Snake folk. He would take a medicine bag with him and it should contain one at least of the new speaking sticks. With it he might acquire a Big Dog.

Donald rubbed his eyes, turned back to where Negog and Jimmy were talking by a bank of driftwood. Something about Jimmy's appearance struck him as unfamiliar. Surely when he last looked at him he had had a yellow splash on his forehead, got no doubt from the newly painted door of Celestin Martel's barn.

HORSE OR GUN?

Which shall I choose of two excellent things,
Big Dog – or the Stick-that-sings?

On Big Dog's back I can eat up the ground,
Faster than antelope, stealthy as hound.
Two-Suns thinks that I hunt remote,
When my knife is a yard from Two-Suns' throat.
The buffalo dream that the plain is clear –
In an hour my bow will twang in their ear.
Who owns Big Dog is a mighty brave,
For the earth is his squaw, and the wind his slave.

With the Stick-that-sings all soft and still
I pick my lair and I make my kill.
Shield nor sentry can cramp the wings
Of the death that flies from the Stick-that-sings.
Man and beast I smite from afar,
And they know not their foe in that secret war.
Big Dog is a marvel beyond dispraise,
But *he* dies at the breath of the Stick-that-slays.

Wherefore, though both are marvellous things,
My voice shall be for the Stick-that-sings.

CHAPTER 7

White Water

Donald had spent two blissful days. There was not much skin left on the palms of his hands, his brow was puffy from the attention of black flies, and nearly every bone in his body ached with weariness. But he had behind him thirty-six hours of delectable memories.

The day before he had started out at dawn with Celestin and Aristide Martel for the Petit Manitou, where the last log drive of the season was concluding. Celestin had a contract with a lumber camp to supply pork and bacon in the coming winter, for his pigs were famous, and there were certain details which he wished to settle. It meant a jog of some twelve miles over a precarious forest road, and Donald's teeth were almost shaken out of his head.

They had breakfast at the lumber camp, that night they slept in the bunkhouse, and for the better part of two days Donald and Aristide were left to their own devices.

Now the Petit Manitou is very different from the Grand Manitou. It flows in a shallow vale among woods of birch and spruce, and, while it has no big waterfall like the other stream, it has a long succession of riffles and pot-holes. Its water is not gin clear, but tinged with peat, and in the pools its hue is dark umber, and in the shallows amber and pale topaz. Its boulder-strewn bed and its endless loops and bends and eddies catch up and becalm the logs, so that at the end of the season it is the job of the lumberjacks with their peevies and pike-poles to set them floating again.

The dam upstream had released a fair head of water, and for two days the drive moved briskly. Sometimes the lumberjacks were in canoes, but mostly they were jumping from boulder to boulder and from log to log with wonderful precision, their caulked boots giving them purchase on the slippery surface. There were no dangerous places in the drive, and though the two boys waited eagerly for a slip they were disappointed. Even when a foothold gave way the man would leap deftly into the air and come down safely on the other side of the rolling log.

It looked simple, but when Donald and Aristide tried the game in a backwater they found it beyond their powers. Their bare feet and prehensile toes could find no grip on the slimy log when it chose to roll, and all day they were as much in the water as out of it. But it was tremendous fun, and when in the evening they turned up at the camp they were forced into dry clothes – shirts and trousers which engulfed them – and Cooky provided a supper which was to remain with both a hallowed memory. There was strong black tea with many spoonfuls of sugar, and smoking bacon and beans, and a choice of many kinds of pie – apple, blueberry, mince, lemon, and custard.

Afterwards in the bunkhouse, when the pipes were lit, they heard talk which thrilled them. Old lumberjacks spoke of White Water. It is the great peril of their lives, but they have no fear of it; they have, so to speak, domesticated it and turned it from an adventure into an art.

Most of the men were from Gaspé, where the habit of the streams is mild, but one or two were from the North Shore, where strong currents flow headlong to the sea from untravelled northern wastes, forcing their way through the rock screens in gigantic cataracts. One man had spent two seasons on the wild Peribonka. But the best tales came from two brothers who had been miners and lumbermen in the Rockies and the Selkirks, and who, more than the others, had the story-telling gift. They drew a picture which caught Donald's imagination – of hundred-mile canyons filled with foaming water, where a man's nerve and strength must last the whole course or death was certain. Once a canoe or a raft was whirled into such a current there was no escape except by completing the job.

The picture filled Donald's thoughts he journeyed homeward. The next afternoon, when he had tea with the Martels, he was unusually silent, so that Father Laflamme, who had also dropped in, remarked on it.

In answer to his question Donald told him about his doings.

"The Company has five hundred men on its payroll," he said, and his voice was solemn with respect.

"Solomon beat it then. He had 80,000 loggers cutting the cedars of Lebanon, and how he got the logs down to the Temple at Jerusalem is what no man knows."

"Did you ever see white water?" Donald asked. "Real white water, I mean. Not like the Manitou, which is either a big waterfall or rapids that anyone can run, but a river which can just be managed if you keep your head and know the game."

"I am lame because of white water," was the answer. "In my time I have seen much white water, and know a little of the art of it. For a man to know it fully he must have been at it all his days."

"There was a fellow at the camp who had been in the West. He said that if you started on the mountain rivers you had to keep going for fifty miles or perish, for there was no place to stop at."

"That I have not seen. My white water lasted at the most for a mile or two. But the art of it is the same everywhere. That must be learned. And also stoutness of heart."

"I think they must be the bravest people in the world," said Donald.

"I will make a confession to you," said Father Laflamme. "Every man has his own particular fear. I was chiefly afraid of being drowned, and since I had to conquer that fear I became expert in avoiding the danger. The best white-water man I have ever known was a Scots half-breed, and he began by being terrified at the gentlest ripple. I think that God has so made us that we can most easily conquer what we are most afraid of – if we have the heart to face up to it."

Father Laflamme accompanied Donald to the water side, where Negog was busy as usual, this time caulking and varnishing one of his salmon cobles. The smell of the varnish seemed to the boy like the smell of the lumber camp, and as he trotted by the priest's side his head was still full of his recent experiences. "White water" had caught his imagination.

He babbled as he twisted from one side of his companion to the other, for Donald moved at a trot, like the caribou, and Father Laflamme's lameness made him slow.

"I can paddle all right," he said, "but I've never tried poling. Which is most difficult? I want to be a river man – a white-water man. How can I learn?"

"Only by experience and taking risks. That is how everything worth while is learned."

"There was a man at the camp who said Aristide and I would train on well. He said we were like Newfoundland dogs, not afraid of the water. That's good for a start, isn't it?"

"I'm not so sure. If you are afraid of a thing you respect it, and if you conquer your fear and keep your respect you will learn how to manage it. There are three things you must not trifle with, you know – that is what the Crees say – first, a bear with cubs, second the sun-glare in your eyes in March, and the third is white water."

Negog heard the last words and laid down his brush.

"The sea trout run tonight," he said, and nodded towards the river.

Donald, much excited, charged down to the nearest pool, but he saw no sea trout...

Instead, he saw a boy standing beside a boat on the grey shingle of a northern island. He looked about sixteen years of age; his freckled face was surmounted by a thatch of hair, bleached almost white by sun and wind; he was tall for his years and had a great breadth of shoulder and length of arm. He wore a fisherman's long knee-boots and a ragged blue jersey. His companion was an elderly man who had lost an arm and, from his features, must have been a kinsman.

That's the end of it," said the boy, "and thank God for that."

"It's maybe not the end, Magnus," said the other. "Man, it's a queer thing that you should have taken this scunner to the sea when your folk for generations have been fishers and never out of boats. It's not as if you were feared o' other things, for you're a fair deevil to fight. I wonder what gave you this grue of salt water?"

"It's any kind of water," said the boy sullenly. "Ay, I'm feared, and that's the plain truth. That's why I'm for Canada, where I'll be a thousand miles from a shore."

"But there's water other places than the ocean," said the older man. "I've heard tell of muckle lakes in Canada and rivers as wide as the Pentland Firth. There was Neil Wabster, I mind, him that went from Kittle Bay, and they were saying he was drowned in some river called by a Hieland name. It seems they go about in wee cockles o' boats, and that there's some awfu' rough water."

The boy shook his head. "There may be water there, but there's plenty land too, and I'm going to bide on the land. I'm off next week. I wish I was across that weariful Atlantic."

The old man shook his head. "Then Orkney will not be seeing you again. Unless," he added with a grin," God Almighty dried up the Atlantic as he dried up the Red Sea for Moses, and that's not very likely...

97

Donald felt that he liked this boy whose name was Magnus Sinclair, and he could see right into his heart. He saw that this son of generations of fishermen and sailors had the one fear which could paralyse an otherwise bold spirit. Death, except by drowning, he was ready to face with coolness, but the horror of deep water and wild water had an icy grip on his heart. It was partly a physical shrinking from a special kind of violence, just as another man fears a wild horse. But the old folks said it was a spell. Magnus's grandfather had seen a mermaid on the skerries and she had laid a curse on him which was now working on his descendant. The village thought no less of Magnus for this shrinking, for he was bold enough in other things; it was an affliction sent from God, like a deaf ear or a blind eye; and the neighbours heartily approved of his plan of going to Canada when the Hudson's Bay Company had their annual summer recruitment.

The course of Magnus's life flowed under Donald's eye like a smooth stream. He saw a scared and sea-sick boy decanted at York Factory on the muddy shore of Hudson's Bay. He saw him in the prentice stage, learning how to judge the furs that the Indians brought in, and what price in "made beaver" should be set on the fruits of their trapping and the store goods supplied to them. Presently Magnus went up-country and was stationed at Norway House, and there he met his old enemy, water, and the struggle began...

He was a good servant to the Company, for he was quick to pick up the Indian tongues, and he could handle discreetly both the Indian trappers and the French *voyageurs*. With the latter, indeed, he was far the most popular of the "Arcanis," as they called the Orkney men. He had a good head for trading, and he was honest as the day, never making up fur *pacquettons* on his own to spoil the Company's business. Indeed, there was nothing in his job which he did not do well, except travel by water. Now and then he had to make a trip with the fur brigades, up the

Saskatchewan or down the Nelson, and once overland to the Churchill and up that river in the long traverse to the Athabasca. When he was only a passenger it was not so bad, for he could avert his eyes from the perils and give all his mind to keeping his nerves still. But sometimes he was in charge of a party, and then it was pure torment, and the boatmen looked anxiously at his distraught eyes, and were puzzled by the tremor in a voice commonly so firm and clear.

He struggled to overcome the fear, but failed lamentably, and lapsed into a mood of sullen resentment against fate. There came a day when his weakness lost his employers a fine load of beaver skins and imperilled the lives of the crew. He was reprimanded and, miserably conscious of his fault, answered rudely and was fiercely taken to task. In a fury, which was directed more against himself than against his masters, he flung up the post and joined the rival North-westers who had long been angling for him.

At first all went well there. His post was far up the Red Deer river in the mountains, and the journeys he had to make were all by land with only inconsiderable hill torrents to ford. But the time came when he was sent north to the Peace river and given charge of all the district between Lake Athabasca and the Rockies. Here most of his movements must be by water, up the Peace, the Smoky, and the Athabasca, even as far as the great Mackenzie, not to mention an infinity of lakes.

And now things came to a crisis. He had begun to feel the pride of achievement and to enjoy the sense of power. Dreams of great enterprises which should conquer for his masters the land beyond the mountains began to hold his mind. But always in the forefront stood the grim barrier of his fear. Until he could vanquish that there was no hope for him; any day he might shipwreck on it, and the Company would send him packing.

He brooded over the matter until something rose in his heart which was stronger than any fear; anger at himself anger and bitter contempt. He resolved to conquer his weakness or flee from the wilds and hide his self-loathing in some humble trade in a landward town.

First he learned to swim, and that was no easy business. He had to conquer his aversion to deep water, and his first attempts convinced him that he must have company to succeed. Now, few of the North-westers, or indeed of the Hudson's Bay people, could swim. Not an Orkney man, for those islanders, who perished generally by drowning, held that swimming only prolonged the agony. Not the French *voyageurs*, whose pride it was to handle boats so that swimming would be needless. Not the Indians, who held that devils lived in deep water and seized a man's legs and pulled him down beside them.

But at last he found two men who had mastered the art. One was Lamallice, a Frenchman from the lower St Lawrence who had learned to swim as a boy among the eel-pots. The other was White Partridge, who, being an Ojibway, came from a country where white water was the rule, and a traveller must learn to ford turbulent streams. In the company of these two Magnus began his course in the backwaters of the Saskatchewan.

He entered the water with a quaking heart, and he was very clumsy while learning from Lamallice the rudiments. But suddenly the whole thing seemed ridiculously easy and familiar. He lost his shrinking from the element and felt at home in it. Presently, with his broad chest and long arms, he developed remarkable skill. Lamallice showed him how to dive, and in a week he had far outdistanced his master, and for a minute or two could explore the floor of the deepest pools. White Partridge taught him how to breast a current, yielding to it, but always stealing an inch or two, and how to let a strong stream carry him down with no damage to limbs. Soon he had as far outdistanced White Partridge as White Partridge at this special game outshone Lamallice. He began to rejoice in the buffeting of rapids and the clutching arms of whirlpools. A river from a menace became a playmate, and an angry river a friend to be humoured and embraced.

Magnus had mastered the first test – to accustom his body and mind to white water. The next was to learn the art by which a man, while remaining in the upper air, could use white water as his servant. For this purpose a heavy York boat was of no use, for their handling was a corporate effort; he had to acquire a private and personal skill. Here Lamallice was an expert, and under his guidance Magnus learned how to thread acres of foam in a birch-bark canoe, and how to pole such a canoe upstream, taking advantage of every patch of shoal water at the edge and every eddy in the main current. He learned how to avoid the deadly peril of a "cellar," where the river flowed over a sunken rock and dropped into a deep pit with sheer glassy sides and a deadly undertow. He learned when boldness was the path of safety. He learned how by a turn of the wrist to shave, with a millimetre to spare, a boulder which would have torn out the side of his canoe. He learned when a floating log might be a menace and when a convenient shelter.

His trips with the fur brigades were no longer nightmares, but seasons of apprenticeship to which he greatly looked forward. He had Lamallice as his chief attendant, and with him he explored faraway waters. He ran most of the Peace rapids above Hudson's Hope, and one of the three pitches where the Slave river becomes a torrent, and a dozen ugly places on the rough trail from the Churchill to the Athabasca. Once on the Nelson river, at the spot now called the Kettle rapids, he made an error in judgment, had his canoe stove in, and was washed up a quarter of a mile downstream with two ribs broken and a wrenched ankle. Lamallice, who helped to pull him out, approved the adventure. "A white-water man," he said, "must three times look death in the face. If he still lives, water is no more a peril to him. You have had your first look."

Then Simon Fraser came upon the scene, and for Magnus the course of life was changed.

Fraser was lean, with a pale skin that no sun or wind could tan, and with dark eyes that had leaping fires in them. His speech was the pleasant singsong of the northern Highlands. For months, at Rocky Mountain House on the Peace river where Magnus was stationed, recruits had been drifting in from the east for a great advance across the mountains which was to carry the Company's front to the western sea. Fraser's first visit was brief. He had two officials of the Company with him, Stuart and McDougall. They crossed the passes and ascended the southernmost of the two rivers which met at the forks, that called the Parsnip, which Alexander Mackenzie had followed a decade earlier. They borrowed Lamallice from Magnus, after they had spent an evening with their pipes and a jorum of rum, thumbing maps and retailing the gossip of the West.

Then for a little Donald saw a wonderful panorama – the shuttles of the pioneers weaving trails across the ranges, posts installed in the high, wild country beyond the Rockies, big lakes where trout could be taken as big as salmon, Indians of a gentler breed than the Plains tribes, and through it all a great river ravening its way south into the iron hills.

There were sallies forth from Rocky Mountain House in spring and autumn, and even in deep winter, till there came a morning in May when the hour struck for the last and boldest enterprise. The river across the Rockies was beyond doubt the great Columbia, whose outlet on the Pacific had been known for two generations. Here lay the true road to the West, a water route, it was said, with few portages, which would bring the rich furs of the coast, the sea otter and the seal, to the North-west depots at Montreal. Nay more, it would enable the Company to trade its furs across the Pacific to the China markets, and bring back tea and silks and rare porcelains – a second East India Company which needed no Government charter.

Simon Fraser, leaner and more sallow than ever, spoke of this to Magnus.

"We'll make your fortune for you, Magnus lad," he said. "We'll set you up as our wintering partner on the coast, and your commission will soon be like a king's ransom. And we need you.

Make your account for that, my dear. This is not a pleasure trip, and God knows what kind of country we'll have to go through before we win to the sea. The Carriers – that's the name they have for the Indians in those parts – say it's one dooms great waterfall, and the folk here tell me you're the best white-water man that ever came out of the North. The thing has been arranged. I've got Duncan McGillivray's instructions for the loan of you in his own hand of write. So it's 'Bundle and go' for you the morn's morn."

In the pleasant spring weather they crossed the Peace river pass, followed the Parsnip to the height of land, and then struck westward to the big lakes called Macleod and Stewart, where Company posts had been set up. Here there was much delay, for a new fort had to be built, and since that year the salmon had failed to run, there was something like a famine among the Indians. In the fall, however, the food supply improved, and it was possible to lay down stores of pemmican and dried fish for the next year's venture. At the tail of winter two Company's men, Quesnel and Farris, came through from Rocky Mountain House with trade goods for barter.

Four stout boats were got together – two of them of bark, and two bigger and heavier dugouts of the kind used by the Haidas on the coast. The canoes were odd things to eastern eyes. Their bark was spruce not birch, and instead of curving bows and sterns they ran out at either end to a point under water. The dugouts were long and narrow to prevent their being swung about by the river eddies. The party numbered twenty-five all told: Fraser himself, Stuart, Quesnel, and Magnus; nineteen *voyageurs*, French and half-breeds, with Lamallice among them; and two Carriers as guides, clad chastely in breech cloths and necklets of grizzlies' claws.

They slipped downstream from the lake posts till they reached a strong river coming down from the north-east at a point where it swung to the south. Fraser laughingly took off his hat to it.

"Hail Columbia!" he said. "We're going to give you a mighty fine chance to drown us. You're a braw river, but there's a wanchancy look about you. You're ower fierce for decency."

Fierce it was, but at the start it was a friendly ferocity which bore the flotilla swiftly, with no need of paddling, from one bivouac to another. The brisk current kept the flies away when camp was made at night on the shore. Food was ample, for the boatmen knocked down many partridges, Magnus' rifle killed a sheep or two and a caribou buck, and the Indians (whom the Frenchmen called Fish Eaters, that being the name of contempt used by the hunting tribes of the Peace for their kin beyond the mountains) set their lines each evening, and there was broiled trout for breakfast.

"This is line travelling," Simon Fraser said, "but it's ower easy. The morn, or maybe the day after, we'll be battling with some infernal Niagara."

The change came suddenly. About noon on the third day the mountains seemed to rush under and choke the river into a funnel. At first the pace of the boats was only quickened; the current ran more fiercely, but still equably, with the even unbroken flow of a gigantic mill-lade. The spirits of the *voyageurs* soared, for the river was doing their work for them, and their boat-songs rose above the drone of the water. But Lamallice's brows were drawn. He saw that the channel was beginning to twist, and he knew that at the turns there would be troublesome eddies.

Sure enough there came a patch of wild water, a sharp-angled precipice, and then a broad reach where the river foamed among boulders and sunken rocks. This was the kind of thing familiar to the *voyageurs*, and they threaded it deftly. But at the next bend the river narrowed into a belt like smooth grey glass. It split at a rock into two streams, each of which dropped in a dizzy glide into a great churning pot. Magnus, who was in the leading canoe, by a lucky instinct took the right-hand stream; if he had taken the other the flotilla must have been cut to pieces on a grid of underwater rock. As it was they were swirled into the right bank, and managed to make fast to its fringe of alders. There was a slender track along the shore, and Stuart, who had charge of the baggage, made them unload and back-pack it, and line the empty boats out of the maelstrom. This took the last three hours of daylight, and it was a wet and weary company that made camp on a spit of gravel, and watched the river burrowing beyond them into the gloom of a still narrower gorge.

Lamallice spoke. "The Fish Eaters say that beyond this it gets worse, and that no man has ever travelled that road. There's still time to go back. There's not much of a shore path but enough to line the bateaux upstream to where we started."

Fraser was peering into the dark.

"What say you, Johnnie?" he asked Stuart, without turning round.

Stuart, prim, neat in his dress, always smacking somewhat of the city, had no doubts.

"I'm for back," he said. "It was a daft-like ploy from the start. What's to hinder this river from flinging itself over a thousand-foot precipice and taking us with it? It's fair suicide to gang on."

"The Indians say there's no big waterfall, only rapids," said Magnus.

"Ay, but they also say that the rapids are ower fearsome for a boat to live in."

Fraser swung round. "We're travelling a road no man has travelled before," he said, "and I'm not denying there's danger in it. I'll drown no man without his consent, so we'd better take a vote."

The vote was equal, the Indians being left out – eleven to go on, eleven to turn back.

"It seems we're a divided house," said Fraser. "Well, the casting vote falls to me, and I give it for going on. There'll be bad bits, and we'll have to make shift to line the boats past them. The Company's credit is in our hands, and, by God! it's not going to suffer by me. We're taking no worse risks than Sandy

105

Mackenzie, and he won through to the Pacific. Providence is on the side of mettled folk."

No one disputed the verdict, for his quiet audacity had laid its spell on the company. That night Magnus slept little, for he knew better than the rest the hazards of the venture. He looked up to the sky, which above the gorge was a thin band of sable, in which the stars burned like hanging lamps with an eerie brilliance. He had faced white water and conquered it – nay, he had made it his friend. But this was the ultimate challenge. There was a curious excitement in his blood, and a tremor, too, at the pit of his stomach. He had moved far since the days when he had lived in dread of the Orkney seas.

He found one of the Carriers beside him sniffing the night air like a dog on the trail.

"We shall get through," he said.

"We shall get through," the Indian repeated, "but not all."

And now Donald with enthralled eyes was a witness of a drama which hourly quickened in speed. He saw not only action and movement, but the hearts of the men – fear rising to resolution or sinking to despair, doubt even in the bravest, and at the back of all Fraser's fatalism and Magnus's doggedness unconsciously supporting the rest. And his other senses were as keen as his eyes. He heard the thunder of the cataracts reverberating between the rock walls, the scream of eagle and fish-hawk, the songs of the *voyageurs* in their scanty hours of rest, and he smelt the bitter odour of broken water, and the incense of the pines and the crags, and the sweetish, sickly smell of the oiled Indians.

Magnus and Lamallice, at bow and stern, were in the first canoe. It was their business to prospect, and if they judged a stretch impossible, to guide the flotilla into the shore and arrange a portage. It was a tricky job, and they made mistakes, avoiding rapids which were reasonably safe and venturing on some which brought them to the edge of disaster. One awful place they encountered on the fifth day, when for nearly two miles the river was constricted to a channel of some thirty yards in which no boat could live for five seconds. On each side the cliffs rose almost sheer, though there was a faint Indian trail among the talus on the right bank. Moreover, they had been warned by the Carriers of unfriendly tribes, and had to post guards on the rock shoulders. The portage was a desperate affair. The boats were lined down, tossing and circling in the whirlpools. The shore trail was widened with hoes, and somehow or other the baggage was carried and the canoes lined past the danger point...

Donald's heart was in his mouth, for a false step would have meant instant destruction. He noticed Fraser descending the cliffs like a mountain goat, for his Highland boyhood had made him sure-footed, and he marvelled to see him driving his dagger into the ground and using it as a handhold...

They reached a place where the cliffs fell back a little, and there they found a settlement of Atnah Indians, who were friendly enough, and provided three horses for the next portage. One of the horses slipped and broke its back on the riverside boulders. There one of the Carriers lost his life, falling into a whirlpool which battered his skull in. The body was recovered, and his companions insisted that the funeral must be in accordance with the custom of his tribe, so they had to retrace their steps to the Atnah village. The Atnahs had the same funeral customs as the Carriers, and the body was burnt with strange incantations... For the first time in his life Donald knew the sickening smell of roasting human flesh...

By this time all the party were ragged and dirty; their nails were half off their fingers, their shoes were in shreds, and their feet and hands were masses of blisters. But Fraser never lost his mastery. He sent scouts ahead to prepare the next batch of Indians for their coming, and when they reached them there was that in his dancing eyes and wild merry face that made them his friends. His face was now so lined that he seemed to be perpetually grinning.

"I've a better notion of handling savages than Mackenzie," he told Magnus. "Sandy couldn't 'gree with the Atnahs, and you saw that they've been eating out of my hand. Sandy was ower much of the dominie."

They reached the land of the Chilcotins and were well received and well fed – fortunately, for after that they had their worst passage. It was a place where portage was impossible, and Magnus decided to trust the thread of glassy current which ran between two maelstroms. It was like a stream in a cave, for the cliffs above narrowed to overhangs which showed only a ribbon of sky. Every man held his breath, as for an hour and more they shot down at a giddy speed, with perdition waiting for them if there was a false paddle stroke. Below that they landed, and all afternoon the crews slept the heavy sleep of men whose nerves had been tried too high.

Fraser shook Magnus's hand.

"Man, you're the grand guide," he said. "I'm content always to follow your judgment, but for myself I'd have said yon place was naked death."

"So would I, if it hadn't been for a fish-hawk. The bird kept on steady in front of me, and I got the notion that it was sent for a good omen."

Fraser laughed.

"Good luck to the bird. But trust your own wits, Magnus, lad. They're safer than freits."

Presently the river became a chain of cascades which no craft could pass. They stowed their boats on a high scaffold in the jack-pines, and each man humped his eighty-pounds weight of baggage. Then began a heart-breaking portage till they reached a camp of the Lilloets, who welcomed them with much hospitable ceremony. Fraser had made his ragged regiment shave and spruce themselves for the occasion. There they procured two canoes and a supply of dried salmon.

Fraser, who had been conferring with the head man, joined the party with a puckered brow.

"I'm puzzled about this damn river," he told Stuart. "These Indians have drawn me a plan of where it enters the sea, and it's not what I have learned of the Columbia's mouth. Maybe we've hit the wrong water."

Next day a strong stream came in on their left, and Fraser was more cheerful. He had heard of it, he said, from David Thompson, for whom it had been named, and it was a tributary tight enough of the Columbia. His good humour was increased by friendly Indians, who traded him sufficient canoes to embark the whole party. And then came an awful ravine where the canoes had to be again abandoned. The portage was for goats, and not for men. Often the trail became a ladder whose sides were poles fixed between trees and boulders...

It was the last of their tribulations. Beyond it the river settled down in its bed and flowed decorously to the sea. Canoes were obtained again, and on the thirty-fifth day of their journey they were in tidal waters.

Fraser took his bearings and sat for a long time in deep thought. Then he beckoned Magnus.

"We're the better part of three degrees ower far north for the Columbia. You and me, we've found a new river."

"We're none the worse for that," was the answer. "We've got to the coast and that was our purpose."

"Ay, but we've found a dooms rough road. The man's mad that would follow our trail. It's not what the Company want, but all the same it's been a mighty great venture. What'll we call our river?"

"The Fraser," was the answer. "There can be but the one name."

"I'm not so sure. I was the leader in name, but you were the leader in truth. I think it might be called the Magnus. Magnus is

Latin for great, and it's a great river... And you're a great man.
You were born without fear."

Magnus laughed happily.

"Not me! I was born with the terror of white water on me.
But I faced it and beat it. And now it's my servant."

Fraser laughed also.

"A very pretty parable," he said. "If I were a minister it would
be a fine tail to a sermon."

Donald saw a sea trout break water in midstream. And then
another. There must be a shoal of them. He blinked his eyes. The
pool was still and golden, but it seemed to him that a second
earlier it had been as choppy as the St Lawrence in a north-easter.

THINGS TO REMEMBER

Child, if you would live at ease
Learn these few philosophies.

If you fear a bully's frown,
Smite him briskly on the crown.
If you're frightened of the dark,
Go to bed without a spark
To light up the nursery stairs,
And be sure to say your prayers.
If your pony's raw and new,
Show that you can stick like glue.
If the fence seems castle-high,
Throw your heart across and try.
Whatsoever risk portends,
Face it and you'll soon be friends.

But though many perils you dare
Mingle fortitude with care.
Do not tempt the torrent's brim
Till you've really learned to swim.
Do not climb the mountain snow
If inclined to vertigo.
Do not let yourself be seen
Mother bear and cubs between;
Or essay your marksman's skill
On a grizzly couched uphill, –
Else this mortal stage you'll leave
And your parents fond will grieve.

111

THE FOOT-TRAVELLER

At first we went on our own flat feet,
    Moccasined, booted, or bare as at birth,
Brisk in frost and laggard in heat,
    Bound for the uttermost ends of the earth.
Hill and prairie and deep muskegs
Were covered in turn by our aching legs.

    We have sailed on the Ultimate Seas,
        We have tramped o'er the Infinite Plain;
    We have carried our pack to the icebergs and back,
        And by —* we will go there again!

We broke the trail on the winter crust,
    Husky and malamute trotting behind;
Our pack-train coughed in the alkali dust,
    And strained in the passes against the wind.
In the prairie loam, on the world's high roof,
From dawn to dusk we padded the hoof.

Canoe and bateau speeded our way,
    But half the time we were wading the creek,
And the longest portage fell on the day
    When our bellies were void and our legs were weak.
Like docile mules we shouldered the pack
And carried a wonderful weight on our back.

---

* Expletive according to taste.

Now behold has a miracle brought
   Ease to our legs and speed to the way;
Outboards chug where canoemen wrought,
   A month's toil now is a morning's play;
The mountain track is a metalled road
And motors carry the pack-train's load.

Through the conquered air we speed to our goal;
   Swamps and forests are dim beneath;
The virgin peak and the untrod Pole
   Fade behind like a frosty breath.
Freed from the toil of our ancient wars,
We outpace the winds and outface the stars.

Yet – when we come to the end of our quest,
   The last grim haul in the gully's heart,
The uttermost ice of the mountain's crest,
   The furthest ridge where the waters part,
The lode deep hid in the cypress fen
A thousand miles from the eyes of men –

Then we return to our fathers' ways,
   For help there is none from earth or heaven;
Once again as in elder days
   We are left with the bodies that God has given.
At the end the first and the last things meet
And we needs must go on our own flat feet.

  We have sailed on the Ultimate Seas,
     We have tramped o'er the Infinite Plain;
  We have carried our pack to the icebergs and back,
     And by — we will go there again!

CHAPTER 8

The Faraway People

One day there was a great bustle at the camp where Donald lived. A telegram had come from his father to Celestin Martel to say that an old friend, one Colonel Bellenden, would spend that night in the camp, and asking him to have an eye to his comfort. So Madame Martel and Simone were busy all afternoon tidying up and arranging for the Colonel's bed and dinner, and Donald a little nervously prepared for his new rôle of host.

The guest arrived at nightfall in a cabin cruiser, which tied up to the little wharf at the Manitou's mouth. He was a huge man of fifty-odd years, who, since he retired from soldiering, had been looking for rare animals in outlandish places. Now his quest was the Arctic char, which in all Quebec was found only in one place, the Grand Lac de Manitou. Celestin Martel had arranged his transport, and next day they were to set out.

It seemed that the Colonel and Father Laflamme had met in the North, and that the Father's cousin and close friend, Charles Monpetit, had been with him in Baffin Land. So Father Laflamme was bidden to dinner, and a very self-conscious boy played host at the head of the table.

Donald had had a heavy day in the sun and wind, and was both hungry and sleepy, but he forgot hunger and drowsiness as he listened to the talk of the two men, for they spoke of secret and wonderful things in the very far North.

114

First they talked of the Arctic char. They argued about its exact kind. Was it the *Salvelinus nitidus*, the shining char of the books? Or a separate species found only in the Grand Lac de Manitou? Anyhow, it was of the same family as was found in the waters of the far North, from Great Bear Lake to Greenland.

"In Baffin Land the Eskimos call it *angmalook*," said Colonel Bellenden. "At least that is their name for a particularly shiny variety of the fish. I've caught it, and I want to see if yours are like it."

"Theocritus described it three centuries ago," said Father Laflamme, and he quoted a Greek line. "Can you translate that, Donald? It means 'the sacred fish that men call silver-white.' "

Then they spoke of how the fish came to be there.

"Left behind from the Ice Age," said the Colonel, "as the ice retired northward. But I'm hanged if I can see how it happened. I suppose that even the Ice Age had some sort of summer and that there were lakes deep enough not to freeze to the bottom. Anyhow, it is a link between our own day and the prehistoric. When it and its kind filled the waters here the Laurentians were not mere rubbed-down stumps but high mountains, and the Appalachians across the river were about the size of Everest."

The talk rambled on until even Donald's interest was overwhelmed by slumber, and he was picked up from the floor by Father Laflamme and carried to bed. But though drunk with sleep he had heard words which made him burrow his head into the pillow in a confused glow of happiness.

The Colonel had said, "The boy seems keen. Why not take him with us tomorrow?"

Donald long remembered the next day's journey. The Martels' buckboard was not the smoothest of vehicles at the best, and the road was a staircase among rocky hills. They had to pass the twenty-mile stretch where the Manitou flowed in deep canyons before they reached the plateau and the tributary which led to the Grand Lac. Donald and Father Laflamme found it more comfortable to walk most of the way.

But at last they came to the Grand Lac, drowsing on its hilltop under a summer sky, and rimmed with woods which at that height still wore their delicate spring green. They had to wait until late afternoon for the rise, when a species of mayfly came in flights over the little bays, and the water boiled with rising fish. Donald had no luck with the Arctic char, for the shining creatures rose swiftly, like a bar of light, and he was too slow on the strike. But he caught a three-pound speckled trout and went to bed happy.

Next day at the morning rise he was more fortunate, and after a sharp tussle brought to the net no less than three of the bright fish, with their tiny scales of very pale gold. Colonel Bellenden also did well, and a contented little company sat down to luncheon, content and comfortable since a light breeze kept the flies at a distance. It was a leisurely meal, for there would be an interval in the fishing till the evening brought the second rise.

They spoke of the far North, and Donald drank in the talk with thirsty ears.

Colonel Bellenden lifted one of the char from the rush-lined creel. Its splendour was slowly dimming, but it was still a wonderful and spectacular thing as contrasted with the brook trout, who is apt to be a dingy object in death.

"The rearguard of the North!" he said. "A gallant rearguard too, for they have been in action for a good many thousand years. You would have to get well down Hudson's Bay before you met these gentry again. There's an extraordinary interest in anything left over from a remote past. Think if we could find a corner where the mammoth still carried on! I've known fellows who thought that possible."

"You're more likely," said Father Laflamme, "to find something of that kind with human beings. They can adapt themselves better to change than animals."

"True. Fifteen hundred years ago we had the Picts in parts of Scotland, little hairy men who fought with stone arrow-heads and had the secret of the heather ale. Some people think that they survived right down almost into our own day, and were the Brownies you hear of in the Galloway moors. There are authentic records of the Brownie there up to about a century ago."

"There may be a survival in Canada. You were at Cape Dorset with Charles Monpetit? Didn't they ever tell you about the Toonits?"

"Yes, by Jove! and I saw one of their houses. They were little chaps like the Picts, weren't they? and lived in stone houses and not in snow igloos and skin tents. If I remember right, they are believed to have been cleaned out a thousand years ago by the present Eskimos, the Tunnit, who came in from the West."

Father Laflamme laughed.

"Charles would not agree to that," he said. "Didn't he tell you of the Eskimo who went hunting in the central plateau towards the Carlos river? Suddenly, up from behind a hillock, pops a little square man with a drawn bow. The Eskimo ran for dear life and never halted till he was back with his tribe a hundred miles off. Charles said he was a dependable man who could neither dream nor lie. He is convinced that up in that forsaken Baffin Land interior there is a Toonit remnant still alive."

"Great Scot!" Colonel Bellenden removed his disgraceful old hat and put a hand through his thinning hair. "There's a yarn for you! Better than the 'Horrible Snow Men' in the Himalayas. A real live Toonit would be enough to drive an anthropologist mad. I must get hold of Monpetit and get details. Where's he to be found?"

"I had a letter from him last week," said Father Laflamme. "He came out about a month ago and at this moment he should be in Quebec. He is not very communicative, but I gather that last winter he had a wild journey in the far north of Baffin Land and pretty nearly came by his end. He says he has a lot to tell me, so perhaps he has seen a Toonit himself."

There was only an hour of fishing left, for they were due to start off home at seven o'clock. Donald caught no more shining fish, but he had several fine speckled trout to his credit. Somehow or other his fishing ardour had ebbed a little. He was alone in a little bight of the lake, and was looking west at a sea of mountains, whose tops were foreshortened, like ships coming over an horizon. The westering sun was on the water, and it was as golden as the back of a char. He was thinking of that wild North of which there had been talk at luncheon.

The gold in the water seemed to change to a murky orange. The sky above was as dead and still as a rock, with no movement of sound or light. The earth below was also dead and motionless. There were tall cliffs of black basalt scarred and puckered with snow, and on their crest a great ice cornice. The sea, too, was puckered and crevassed since the wind had driven the ice pack against the shore. Ice cap above and ice pack below, and between cliff and sea a snow-slabbed beach. It was desperately cold, forty or fifty below zero. Donald, by the shore of that sunlit lake, did not feel the cold, but his other senses were alive to it; he *saw* it – the cruel orange firmament, the unearthly stillness, the colourless world. There was something terrible about the icy cupola of sky, which was ruddy like a flame.

A little party of men was making its way along the shore, and the strange thing was that Donald knew all about them. There were twelve dogs in the team that drew the sledge, and an Eskimo driver, whose name was Ecka-look, or The Trout, and who by a turn of the wrist could, with his twenty-foot whip, remind a dog of its duty. Another Eskimo, Pitsulak, or The Sea Pigeon, went on in front to break the trail. In the rear walked a tall figure, which Donald knew was Charles Monpetit, the Oblate Father who was a cousin of his own Father Laflamme. He was dressed in sealskin pants over corduroy breeches, the long boots called kamiks, with soles made from the square-flapper seal and uppers of ordinary sealskin, thick duffel stockings, woollen shirt below a dickey of caribou skin, and on his head a parka with the face opening lined with wolverine fur.

The place was the south coast of Cornwall Island, well inside the Arctic Circle, the month was February, the hour was three in the afternoon, and the sun was just dropping below the horizon. Monpetit was on his way to the remote station of Fripp Inlet to visit and succour a brother missionary, for word had come down the coast by some mysterious moccasin telegraph that the priest at Fripp was gravely ill, and since Monpetit was the only man with any medical knowledge within a thousand miles it was his duty to go to his aid. Already he had been five days on the road, and if the fates were kind and the weather held he should reach his goal in another two.

The orange sky suddenly became a dull slaty-blue, and the light seemed to go out of the landscape. The team stopped automatically, the dogs were unharnessed and rolled in the snow, and the Eskimos took out their snow knives and began to cut blocks for an igloo.

"This is a good place," said Ecka-look. "There will be no wind, I think. If it blows it will be from the north, and the cliff is therefore a shelter."

Monpetit, who knew something of the awful power of an Arctic blizzard, nodded in assent.

Once the igloo in which he slept had been wrapped by a blizzard in a four-foot covering of snow, so that all air vents were blocked, and but for his lucky awakening with bursting lungs the party must have perished... But as, in the failing light, he looked at the cliff behind him and saw far up the edge of an overhanging snowfield he did not feel so certain about the merits of the site. He was mountain bred, and in Dauphine in such a place there might be an avalanche or an ice-fall.

The last light had scarcely gone before the igloo was completed. There was no special shelter built for the dogs, as is the Greenland fashion, but they were left to camp in the snow after their meal of frozen fish. The runners of the sledge were seen to, and scraped into an even convex, which before starting next day would be further lubricated by being given a fresh skin of ice. Inside the igloo the two primus stoves were set going, whence came a faint light, and presently a real warmth. On racks placed above them each man hung his wet clothing. On one stove snow was melted in a kettle to make tea; and the other was filled with fragments of frozen beans and ship's biscuit. Soon the place was as warm and steamy as a vapour bath, and the Eskimos, as sensitive to heat as any white man, stripped off their dickeys.

Supper did not take long, and presently the two Eskimos were asleep. But Monpetit was wakeful, for a long day's journey tired him more than his companions, and he had to wait until his body could sink into apathy. The igloo was full of tiny noises, the sputterings of the stoves and the drip of moisture from roof and walls. But soon he grew used to them and they became the background against which other noises stood out. His hearing became unnaturally keen to detect any stirrings outside.

All day in that world of deathly silence he had been conscious of the monotonous sounds of travel. There was the steady thump of the dogs' feet coming out of the orange cloud made by their breath. There was the sound of the runners on the snow – a sharp hissing when the snow was hard, and where it was soft a kind of cotton-wool slushing. Now these noises had gone out of his ears and he was hearing new ones.

There was a steady patter of the dogs' feet as they prowled round the igloo. They always did that after being fed, in quest, perhaps, of a further meal before they settled down in their cold lairs.

Presently that stopped, and was succeeded by a multitude of queer little sounds. One was a gentle drip which came from the outside, like the noise of snow slipping from the eaves of a house. There was a clattering, too, as if little bits of ice were falling. This puzzled Monpetit, for there was no wind and the night was dead calm. It must be a fall of ice fragments from the cliff behind them. But what, in that stricture of frost, made the fragments fall? He did not like it; it reminded him of his own unpredictable ice-wreathed Dauphine peaks.

Then he heard something which puzzled him more. It was the sound of feet. Not dog's paws, but feet, human or of some biggish animal. There were no human beings within a hundred miles, and at that season there could be no caribou or musk ox on the shore. A bear? But the sound had not the shuffle of a bear. Monpetit's mind sprang into full wakefulness and sharp anxiety. Thank heaven the Eskimos were asleep! If they heard it they would panic about the Ghost Sledge, or some other of their many bogey tales...

Donald in his picture saw both the inside and the outside of the igloo, and what he saw outside startled him, though in the black night it was only a dance of shadows.

People were there – how many he could not tell, but not less than half a dozen. There was no sign of how they had come, no dogs, no sledge, they had simply welled out of the darkness. They were small people – of that he was certain – smaller than the Eskimos in the igloo, much smaller than Monpetit; and they did not move like ordinary mortals, but with a queer shuffling step like a bear.

What were they doing? They seemed able to see like cats in the dark, for they had spotted the igloo at once and were padding round it. They stopped to sniff, too, like dogs; they were conscious of the smell of humanity close at hand. They seemed to halt and take counsel. Then one of them plucked from somewhere on his person a crooked thing like a scimitar. He brandished it in the air and then plunged it in the igloo's side at a joint between the blocks of snow.

Suddenly the whole party sprang backward and raised their heads. Something was happening on the cliff. Even in the darkness Donald was conscious of a huge moving curtain slipping down with the sound which water makes when it falls from a height so great that it is mostly spent in spray. It seemed to him that the igloo, whose outline he felt rather than saw, was suddenly raised to a conical tower. The little figures that surrounded it disappeared like rabbits at the report of a gun. Slowly the curtain drooped and then it seemed to stop and lie draped in thick folds along the flat...

Monpetit in the igloo listened anxiously to the padding of feet – mortal feet. He was muttering a prayer automatically, but every nerve in his brain was alive. His fear was human, not panic, which is animal. There was something outside which was man and with which man could deal... And then he remembered the tale of the Eskimo on the Carlos river. The Toonits? The aboriginal folk of the North who had disappeared for a thousand years? Was he fated, here in the ends of the earth, to encounter the last earth-dwellers? For a second a strong intellectual curiosity steadied his nerves.

It enabled him to hear a new noise. The clatter of ice fragments suddenly stopped and was replaced by a steady drone, as if something soft and weighty were crushing down on something solid... Now he knew where he was. He had heard that sound in a bivouac on the Meije. The ice cap on the cliff had slipped and the igloo was in the track of an avalanche.

Luckily he had not removed his dickey. With two violent kicks he awoke his companions into consciousness, then he dived at the wall nearest the sea and forced his hundred-and-eighty pounds through it. He had seen this done before in Baffin Land and a happy chance brought it to his memory... Into the black night tumbled a dishevelled Oblate Father, closely followed by two half-clad Eskimos.

The change from the steamy igloo to the dry, bitter night was so harsh that for a moment Monpetit was half paralysed. He drew breath through clenched teeth, for the cold was enough to freeze his lungs. Thank God he had his dickey! But he had no protection for his head, and he had only one mitt. The Eskimos had nothing – parka, dickey, mitts, nor kamiks – only their shirts and pants and duffel stockings. All three were at the mercy of a winter night and would soon be dead.

Monpetit saw that the avalanche had stopped. It had submerged the igloo, but, so far as he could judge, had not crushed it. It had blocked up the hole in the wall through which he had escaped. Inside were clothes and warmth. Unless they could get inside they would assuredly perish.

But how? They had no snow knives, no implement but their naked hands. Monpetit made for the point where they had emerged and found a curtain of avalanche snow which must be at least four feet thick. It was still softish, though soon it would harden into ice. He tore at it with his single mitt, and the Eskimos tore at it with their naked hands, but they could only clutch small handfuls. It was like a bird scrabbling with helpless claws against a stone wall...

He felt his strength ebbing under the impact of the cold. Worse, the exertion made him pant, and he was in terror of drawing ice into his lungs. He was a brave man, but he felt his manhood being squeezed out of him by the cruel grip of the North. He wanted to sink back into apathy or prayer, which would mean death...

And then suddenly he felt something hard below his knees, and out of the snow he drew a knife.

It was such a snow knife as he had never seen before, curved like a scimitar, made of bone or ivory, and curiously grooved and fluted. But it was what he needed. With it he hewed great chunks out of the drift that draped the igloo wall. Soon he had reached the wall itself and could scoop out easily the soft snow which now filled the hole he had made. A refreshing waft of heat came out to greet him. The two Eskimos were shoved through first, for their need was the greater, and lay panting on the floor like newly speared seals.

Monpetit, as soon as he got his breath, knelt beside the others and gave fervid thanks for the miracle which had been vouchsafed him. God had interfered directly with His grace to save His servant's life by providing out of the void an instrument of salvation. He examined the heavenly gift. If it was of angel workmanship, then the celestial folk followed closely mortal patterns, for he recognised in the delicate incised work various Eskimo conventions. The blade was long, but the handle was very small, as if meant for tiny hands... He remembered the sound of human feet which he had heard outside the igloo before the avalanche.

Donald blinked hard, for he was looking straight into the eye of the sun, which was now far down in the west. He wondered, not for the first time, why excessive light should be so near darkness, for it seemed to him that he had been for a moment or two in the dark.

As they jogged home in Celestin Martel's buckboard Father Laflamme remembered something else about his friend in the North.

"Charles tells me," he said, "that he is bringing back a wonderful curiosity. It is a snow knife he found in Cornwall Island. He thinks it may be Toonit workmanship."

Father Monpetit duly came to Petit Fleurs a few weeks later, and Donald heard from his own lips the story of his miraculous escape from the avalanche. He saw, too, and handled, the snow knife which had been the instrument of Heaven. The Father was positive that its origin was Toonit.

"It lay there on the shore," he said, "for a thousand years till the moment came for it."

"Isn't it a bit younger than a thousand years?" Donald asked. "It seems fairly new. Might not there still be some Toonits up there who only lost it the other day?"

The Father looked curiously at the boy. "Maybe," he said. "God is great."

In the following winter Donald's form master at school gave his class a talk one afternoon about the story of exploration in the North. It was a rather good talk, beginning with old Henry Hudson and going down through Baffin and Hearne and the pirate D'Iberville to Franklin and Parry and Rae and Back, and the Hudson's Bay Company who today are using the North-west Passage of which Amundsen was the pioneer, and which was sought for five hundred years. He spoke also of the Eskimos who, he said, had come from Asia over the Behring Strait. Upon this Donald had raised the question of the Toonit, about whom the master was more than sceptical. Donald, I fear, argued his case with such vigour that he was accused of disrespect, and was given a hundred lines of *Paradise Lost* as an imposition to improve his manners!

QU'APPELLE?

Qu'appelle?
A whisper steals through the sunburnt grasses;
Faint as a twilight wind it passes,
    Broken and slow,
    Soft and low,
And the heart responds like a beaten bell;
For the voice comes out of the ancient deeps
Where the blind, primordial Terror sleeps,
And hark! It is followed by soft footfalls!
    Who calls?

Qu'appelle?
What is it stirs the cedars high,
When there is no wind in all the sky,
    And plays queer tunes
    On the saskatoons,
Subtler airs than the ear can tell?
The evening breeze? But wise men warn
That the tune and the wind are elfin-born,
And lure the soul to uncanny things.
    Who sings?

Qu'appelle?
The world is empty of stir and sound,
Not a white fox barks in the void profound;
    On the Elder Ice
    Old Silence lies,

Older than Time and deep as Hell.
Yet a whisper creeps as a mist from a fen
Which is not the speech of articulate men,
And the hunter flees like a startled bird.
    Whose word?

EPILOGUE

John Buchan thought that history was too often taught to children in such a way that they found it a dull subject. He said that they must be told stories and legends about what had happened in their own country, in order to awaken an interest in their ancestors.

So he set to work to try and show Canadian children how romantic and exciting he felt the history of Canada to be. In this book he has mixed new times with olden times. Donald, who is not at all good at learning history at school, suddenly has it brought before his eyes in a series of magic pictures. John Buchan was aware that some Indians have the power of projecting happenings of long ago on to a piece of calm water; so he chose Negog, the Indian, Donald's companion and guide, to wave a magic wand over the past, and we see a rich pageant moving before our eyes as we turn over the pages of this book.

Among the author's papers I found a chapter called "Trusty and Well-beloved," which he did not quite finish. On the wall of the sitting-room in Donald's home hung his father's commission in the Militia, which said that His Majesty called on the services of an officer whom he described as "trusty and well-beloved." These words strongly impressed Donald's fancy. They seemed to him to be the highest terms of compliment possible in the English language. He applied them at various times to his own belongings – a cocker spaniel and a catapult, among other things! It seemed to him that the words also applied to Tim

Haskins, who had done everything which seemed to the boy worth doing. He had trapped, traded, and prospected down the Mackenzie river, and something about Tim's steady grey eyes always recalled the phrase to him.

This story tells of how Tim Haskins and Father Laflamme were talking together. Donald listened for a time and then slipped off to the river to see how the fish were running. He found Negog beside the Sea-pool mending a net that was used for sprats. The Indian looked up from his work, nodded, and bent to it again.

"Fish running?" Donald asked.

"One – two – three. Not many fish. I think the weather changes. Tomorrow will be rain and wind." He looked up to the cloudless evening sky, turned his head eastward, and sniffed the air.

"Storm comes," he said. Then he grinned and added something which Donald did not understand. "After tonight there will not be the Long Traverse."

So this is how "The Long Traverse" ends. The manuscript breaks off a few pages later, but before it ends it tells how Donald sees a vision of Tim Haskins, twenty years younger, just before the outbreak of the first Great War in 1914. He sees Tim in the North with a half-breed called Andy Applin. They had made camp in a little bay where the sand was grey like granite. Supper was nearly over, mugs of coffee were being handed round, and pipes were alight. With them were three college boys from Michigan, metallurgical students who were doing a bit of practical prospecting. They were looking for gold, and going off to a place called Blue Heron Lake. Tim shows them a sample of vari-coloured sand, amongst which is some yellow stuff rather like sulphur. He tells them that it is pitchblende, in which radium is found.

While Tim is explaining that he and Andy are going off to look for more pitchblende they hear the sound of a canoe's paddle, and see a canoe with a solitary figure in it coming along.

Andy cries out that it is Bill Macrae, the Mounty. The boys greet him and give him flapjacks and coffee. While he is eating he breaks the news to them that Britain is fighting Germany.

Without a moment's hesitation Tim and Andy announce that they intend to go and fight, and are soon headed south, for there is no time to spare if they want to beat the freeze-up.

The manuscript ends here, but John Buchan had already written the whole story of the discovery of pitchblende, and some day you may see it depicted in a film.

John Buchan

Castle Gay

Retired Glasgow provisions merchant and adventurer, Dickson McCunn, first seen in *Huntingtower*, features for a second time in *Castle Gay*. His group of boys known as the Gorbals Die-hards have gone on to Cambridge University. Now Dougal and Jaikie embark on 'seeing the world'. Their escapades involve Castle Gay, its occupant Mr Craw, and all manner of interesting characters.

The Free Fishers

Set in the bleak Yorkshire hamlet of Hungrygrain, this is a stirring tale of treason and romance. Anthony Lammas, minister and Professor of Logic at St Andrews University finds himself entangled in a web of intrigue that threatens the country. His boyhood allegiance to a brotherhood of deep-sea fishermen involves him and his handsome ex-pupil with a beautiful but dangerous woman.

John Buchan

Greenmantle

Sequel to The Thirty-nine Steps, this classic adventure is set in war-torn Europe. Richard Hannay, South African mining engineer and hero, is sent on a top-secret mission across German-occupied Europe. The result could alter the outcome of World War I. Other well-known characters make a reappearance here: Sandy, Blenkiron and Peter Pienaar.

Huntingtower

Dickson McCunn is a retired Glasgow provisions merchant who sets out to find adventure in *Huntingtower*. He is benefactor of the Gorbals Die-hards, a group of poor boys who have formed their own version of a Boy Scout troop.

John Buchan

Prester John

After his father's death our young hero sets off to make his fortune in South Africa. He gets tangled up in an African tribal uprising and the strange encounter and rumours he hears along his journey make him suspect that his destination may not be as predictable as he has supposed. Set at the turn of the last century, this is a real adventure story.

The Thirty-nine Steps

John Buchan's most famous and dramatic novel presents spy-catcher Richard Hannay. Hannay is in London when he suddenly finds himself caught up in a dangerous situation and the main suspect for a murder committed in his own flat. He is forced to go on the run to his native Scotland.

TITLES BY JOHN BUCHAN AVAILABLE DIRECT
FROM HOUSE OF STRATUS

Quantity		£	$(US)	$(CAN)	€
FICTION					
	THE BLANKET OF THE DARK	6.99	11.50	15.99	11.50
	CASTLE GAY	6.99	11.50	15.99	11.50
	THE COURTS OF THE MORNING	6.99	11.50	15.99	11.50
	THE DANCING FLOOR	6.99	11.50	15.99	11.50
	THE FREE FISHERS	6.99	11.50	15.99	11.50
	THE GAP IN THE CURTAIN	6.99	11.50	15.99	11.50
	GREENMANTLE	6.99	11.50	15.99	11.50
	GREY WEATHER	6.99	11.50	15.99	11.50
	THE HALF-HEARTED	6.99	11.50	15.99	11.50
	THE HOUSE OF THE FOUR WINDS	6.99	11.50	15.99	11.50
	HUNTINGTOWER	6.99	11.50	15.99	11.50
	THE ISLAND OF SHEEP	6.99	11.50	15.99	11.50
	JOHN BURNET OF BARNS	6.99	11.50	15.99	11.50
	THE LONG TRAVERSE	6.99	11.50	15.99	11.50
	A LOST LADY OF OLD YEARS	6.99	11.50	15.99	11.50
	MIDWINTER	6.99	11.50	15.99	11.50
	THE PATH OF THE KING	6.99	11.50	15.99	11.50
	THE POWER-HOUSE	6.99	11.50	15.99	11.50
	PRESTER JOHN	6.99	11.50	15.99	11.50
	A PRINCE OF THE CAPTIVITY	6.99	11.50	15.99	11.50
	THE RUNAGATES CLUB	6.99	11.50	15.99	11.50

ALL HOUSE OF STRATUS BOOKS ARE AVAILABLE FROM GOOD BOOKSHOPS OR
DIRECT FROM THE PUBLISHER:

Internet: **www.houseofstratus.com** including author interviews, reviews, features.

Email: **sales@houseofstratus.com** please quote author, title and credit card details.

TITLES BY JOHN BUCHAN AVAILABLE DIRECT
FROM HOUSE OF STRATUS

Quantity	£	$(US)	$(CAN)	€
FICTION				
SALUTE TO ADVENTURERS	6.99	11.50	15.99	11.50
THE SCHOLAR GIPSIES	6.99	11.50	15.99	11.50
SICK HEART RIVER	6.99	11.50	15.99	11.50
THE THIRTY-NINE STEPS	6.99	11.50	15.99	11.50
THE THREE HOSTAGES	6.99	11.50	15.99	11.50
THE WATCHER BY THE THRESHOLD	6.99	11.50	15.99	11.50
WITCH WOOD	6.99	11.50	15.99	11.50
NON-FICTION				
AUGUSTUS	20.00	33.00	48.95	33.50
THE CLEARING HOUSE	8.99	14.99	22.50	15.00
GORDON AT KHARTOUM	8.99	14.99	22.50	15.00
JULIUS CAESAR	8.99	14.99	22.50	15.00
THE KING'S GRACE	8.99	14.99	22.50	15.00
THE MASSACRE OF GLENCOE	8.99	14.99	22.50	15.00
MONTROSE	10.99	17.99	26.95	18.00
OLIVER CROMWELL	12.99	20.99	34.95	21.00
SIR WALTER RALEIGH	10.99	17.99	26.95	18.00
SIR WALTER SCOTT	10.99	17.99	26.95	18.00

ALL HOUSE OF STRATUS BOOKS ARE AVAILABLE FROM GOOD BOOKSHOPS OR
DIRECT FROM THE PUBLISHER:

Hotline: UK ONLY: **0800 169 1780**, please quote author, title and credit card details.
INTERNATIONAL: **+44 (0) 20 7494 6400**, please quote author, title, and
credit card details.

Send to: **House of Stratus Sales Department**
24c Old Burlington Street
London
W1X 1RL
UK

Please allow for postage costs charged per order plus an amount per book as set out in the tables below:

	£(Sterling)	$(US)	$(CAN)	€(Euros)
Cost per order				
UK	2.00	3.00	4.50	3.30
Europe	3.00	4.50	6.75	5.00
North America	3.00	4.50	6.75	5.00
Rest of World	3.00	4.50	6.75	5.00
Additional cost per book				
UK	0.50	0.75	1.15	0.85
Europe	1.00	1.50	2.30	1.70
North America	2.00	3.00	4.60	3.40
Rest of World	2.50	3.75	5.75	4.25

PLEASE SEND CHEQUE, POSTAL ORDER (STERLING ONLY), EUROCHEQUE, OR INTERNATIONAL MONEY ORDER (PLEASE CIRCLE METHOD OF PAYMENT YOU WISH TO USE) MAKE PAYABLE TO: STRATUS HOLDINGS plc

Cost of book(s): _____ Example: 3 x books at £6.99 each: £20.97

Cost of order: _____ Example: £2.00 (Delivery to UK address)

Additional cost per book: _____ Example: 3 x £0.50: £1.50

Order total including postage: _____ Example: £24.47

Please tick currency you wish to use and add total amount of order:

☐ £ (Sterling)   ☐ $ (US)   ☐ $ (CAN)   ☐ € (EUROS)

VISA, MASTERCARD, SWITCH, AMEX, SOLO, JCB:

☐ ☐ ☐ ☐ ☐ ☐ ☐ ☐ ☐ ☐ ☐ ☐ ☐ ☐ ☐ ☐ ☐ ☐ ☐ ☐

Issue number (Switch only):

☐ ☐ ☐

Start Date: **Expiry Date:**

☐☐ / ☐☐   ☐☐ / ☐☐

Signature: _____

NAME: _____

ADDRESS: _____

_____

POSTCODE: _____

Please allow 28 days for delivery.

Prices subject to change without notice.
Please tick box if you do not wish to receive any additional information. ☐

House of Stratus publishes many other titles in this genre; please check our website (**www.houseofstratus.com**) for more details.